THE CABIN, THE NURSE, LIFE CHANGES

Donna M Bryan

Copyright © 2015 Donna M Bryan

This is a book of fiction. Names, characters, and incidents are products of the author's imagination. Any resemblance to actual events, locales, or persons living or dead, is entirely coincidental.

All rights reserved.

ISBN: 1512289337
ISBN-13: 978-1512289336

Cover image curtesy of artist Ellen Tylka.
For more information about Ellen's art and paintings,
email: tylkael@gmail.com

Many thanks to my friends and fellow writers;
Claudia, Marlene, Teri, Janet and Mary, and to those who have been there to listen.
Special thanks to my talented daughter, Brenda Marsolek, who made this possible by assembling the written word for publishing. Without her the book would still be unpublished.
Thanks also to artist Ellen Tylka for doing the cover art.
I've been asked where I get my story ideas. They just come to me, a lot of time in the early morning hours. Then when I start to type, they just expand.

Cast of Characters

Cody Harris – undercover CIA
Susan Harris – deceased wife of Cody
Beth Harris – four-year old twin daughter
Bobbi Jo Harris – four-year old twin daughter
Andrew – son
Buddy – collie dog

Kayla Egan – teacher/nanny

Hal Johnson/Reid – Cody's undercover partner
Betty and Dave Wilson – Hal's sister and husband
Janine – five-year old niece of Hal
Marla – three-year old niece of Hal
Lee – factious roommate

Dr. Conrad Deerwater (The Chief) – facial reconstruction surgeon
Dr. Paul Armstrong – assistant surgeon
Karen – nurse, friend
Jerry – anesthesiologist
Jean – nurse

Sierra – Dr. Deerwater's cousin, cook/housekeeper
Joe – Sierra's husband, physical therapist, jack of all trades
Running Eagle – Indian Shaman

Father Jim – Catholic Priest

Captain Marlin – in charge of CIA division
Shelly – waitress under cover CIA

Dean – Shelly's partner CIA

Patricia O'Malley – sister of Ted
Ted O'Malley

Greg – medic
Dr. Merick
Nurse Kip

Warden Sands
Agent Williams
Agent Lopez
Harry – body guard (tall/slim)
James – body guard (short/blond)

<u>Criminals</u>
Big Jake – drug smuggler leader
Roberto
Frenchy
Lennie
Carmine

Ardie – drug dealer different group
Frankie – Ardies right hand man

Hank – drug dealer
Ronco – drug dealer

CONTENTS

Chapter One: The Shiny Monster 9
Chapter Two: Pie and Guns 18
Chapter Three: Voice Behind the Door 24
Chapter Four: Target Practice and the Truth 28
Chapter Five: The Partner 36
Chapter Six: Gunfire 44
Chapter Seven: Kayla In Action 49
Chapter Eight: Many Thoughts 56
Chapter Nine: Emotions 61
Chapter Ten: Beth Hurts 66
Chapter Eleven: The Phone Call 71
Chapter Twelve: Injured 76
Chapter Thirteen: Mystery at the Mine 88
Chapter Fourteen: The Hospital 94
Chapter Fifteen: Prison Talk 100
Chapter Sixteen: Villains Strike Again 104
Chapter Seventeen: Merry Christmas 111
Chapter Eighteen: The Letter 119
Chapter Nineteen: Mr. Jones 123
Chapter Twenty: The Lodge 129
Chapter Twenty-One: First Day Of Recovery 134
Chapter Twenty-Two: Remove the Casts 141
Chapter Twenty-Three: The Walk 149
Chapter Twenty-Four: Entertainment 154
Chapter Twenty-Five: Bad Memories 160
Chapter Twenty-Six: The Healing Begins 169
Chapter Twenty-Seven: The Truth Revealed 174
Chapter Twenty-Eight: Dr. Deerwater 178
Chapter Twenty-Nine: Visit with Ted 183
Chapter Thirty: Conrad Picks a Nurse 188
Chapter Thirty-One: Wedding Plans 193

Chapter Thirty-Two: Wedding Plans Continue 197
Chapter Thirty-Three: The Guests Arrive 202
Chapter Thirty-Four: Man Talk 211
Chapter Thirty-Five: The Wedding 216
ABOUT THE AUTHOR 223
OTHER BOOKS BY DONNA M BRYAN 224

"The Monster"

CHAPTER ONE

The Shiny Monster

Returning from her short walk in the woods behind the cabin, Kayla filled her arms with chopped wood from the pile and walked slowly balancing the bulky load. Carefully maneuvering the two steps onto the porch, she kicked her brown leather boot against the wooden door. "Open the door! This armful of wood is heavy!"

Not hearing any noise from the cabin indicated help wasn't coming. As she twisted around trying to pull the latch strap, the logs fell on her feet.

"Ouch!" Kayla hopped first on one foot, then the other to ease the pain. "I thought these boots were supposed to protect my feet. I bet all my toes are broken." Sitting down on the top step, she tugged off the boots, afraid her toes might still be in them.

Massaging first one foot, then the other, she looked around wondering where everyone was. All Kayla could hear were the birds singing out their melodies and the wind gently blowing through the trees, soothing and familiar.

From across the clearing, Buddy, the honey colored collie, bounded toward her with the energy dogs have. He stopped by her feet, put his paws on Kayla's lap, and happily licked her face in greeting. Putting her arms around the friendly dog, she buried her face in his soft fur.

Looking up, she watched as Cody and his twin daughters, Beth and Bobbi Jo, emerged laughing from the forest, each carrying their treasure find of the day.

Was it only a month ago she had answered the ad for a teacher/nanny? Two weeks later and here she was, in a cabin over a day away from any neighbors, trying to help the four year old girls deal with the loss of their mommy. Kayla sighed. She knew their daddy was still dealing with the death even though he did try to conceal it.

It had only been six months. Time heals all wounds they say. She wondered how long it took since she still missed her beloved grandmother who raised her after her folks had died.

Kayla gingerly stood up as the three approached the porch.

Beth and Bobbi Jo ran up the steps, both talking at once, explaining what was in their bags.

Bending down, Kayla put an arm around each girl. "Beth, Bobbi Jo, one at a time, I can't understand either one of you when you both talk at once."

They sat down on the steps, one on each side of her. "We had fun finding those white things that Daddy said will taste like potatoes when they are cooked." Bobbi Jo opened her knapsack and picked out some roots.

Beth opened her little bag and pulled out an apple. "Daddy said maybe you could make us an apple pie. He loves apple pie." She looked up at Kayla. "You do know how to make pies don't you? Mommy always made Daddy pies."

Visions of the old iron cook stove that she was still getting acquainted with, and not knowing how to adjust the heat of the oven, danced across her mind, making Kayla feel ever so inadequate for living in the wild. And now a request for a homemade pie that would be baked in the monster stove. She sure hoped there was a recipe for one in the cook book she brought along with her other books.

Putting her arms around the girls, she looked up at Cody. "Why, I think making pies would be fun, but you all have to help me, okay?"

Kayla saw a look of relief show on Cody's face.

"Are you okay, Kayla? It looks like you had a bit of a spill here." Cody remarked glancing at the scattered pieces of kindling over the porch and her boots. He bent down quickly gathering them up. What had been a huge armful for Kayla fit easily in one of his.

"Well, the feeling is back in my toes, but I may wear my bedroom slippers the rest of the day." She gave him a rueful smile.

"We're hungry, Kayla. Is lunch ready yet?" The girls tugged on her hands, and Buddy sat on his haunches and raised both paws.

Picking up her boots, Kayla replied, "Yes, I have a nice soup simmering on the stove. While you wash your hands, I'll dish up the soup and we can all eat."

"I'm really hungry after all the walking we did. You didn't burn anything today did you, Kayla?" Beth asked innocently. Even at her young age she realized that the 'monster' as Kayla called the stove, was still a challenge for Kayla to cook on.

Kayla gave a small laugh. "No, I didn't burn anything so far today. As a matter of fact, let's hope everything in the soup is cooked!"

The girls giggled as they washed their hands in the basin.

Kayla glanced over to Cody's room as he carried a still heavy bag into his room. *Um, he removed apples earlier from that bag. Was he saving some for another day? It seemed that every other day he went into his room with objects in his knapsack. Yet she never saw him bring anything back out. He also told her that no one could enter his room. He would clean it himself; like she could go in if she wanted to. He kept a lock on the door and had the only key. Oh well, I was hired to take care of the girls, not worry about their daddy.*

***

Cody leaned against the door frame watching Kayla, who stood frowning with her arms folded as she contemplated the stove. He felt a twinge of guilt for not elaborating on the primitive conditions out here when he ran the ad and interviewed her. He needed someone like her to be with his girls, and was afraid she would refuse to take the position just as the other five applicants had, after he told them exactly, no hedging, on how primitive it would be.

He made the decision to gloss over the few facts she needed to know when he saw how his daughters took to Kayla, and she responded to them. It was uncanny how similar she was like Susan with Bobbi Jo and Beth. The twins were all he had now. But would Kayla be able to handle the loneliness and hardships of this remote land and stay until spring? He sure hoped so.

Cody pushed away from the door and approached Kayla. "No matter how long you stare at that stove, it will not magically turn into an electric range." He smiled at her.

"What if I go through the instructions again about which kind of wood to use and how to adjust the damper?"

"That would be nice, but will you write it down for me to look over later? Just put it by the burn cream and Band-Aids." She looked at her hands that had already made contact with various spots on the hot stove. *But she had to admit, she was learning. It was called 'trial and error' resulting in a lot of errors. No way was this monster going to win. Oh, what she wouldn't give for the nice white electric stove sitting so prim and proper back at her apartment. Make that electric all over the cabin. If wishes were dollars, she'd be one rich lady by the time she left this wilderness.*

Cody laughed. "You're doing a grand job with the cooking especially for someone who has never cooked on a wood burning range before. As I walk you through this, we can get the oven warmed up to the right temperature for the pies. You did plan on making the pies this afternoon didn't you?"

The look on his face reminded Kayla of a young boy wanting a special treat.

"Of course, if I get some help peeling the apples while I make the crusts." Kayla smiled. Just having him get the monster ready made her happy.

Kayla noticed some yawns from the girls. "Hey, my pretties are you going to help make the pies, or do you need a nap after the long walk today?"

Cody bent down and picked up his daughters, one in each arm. "Why don't I tuck you in for a short rest? You don't have to sleep, just lie there awhile. I'll help Kayla with the apples, and when the pies are done, both of you can be the taste testers."

"Yes, Daddy, I want to be a taste tester." Beth replied.

Nodding her head, Bobbi Jo yawned. "Me too."

Cody carried his tired daughters into their room, tucked them in and gave each one a kiss before returning to the kitchen. Rolling up his sleeves, he looked at Kayla. "Where do you want me to start Ole Mistress of the Kitchen?"

"I've washed the apples, so you can peel them, take out the core and slice them or just core and slice them. They don't have pesticides on them to worry about." Kayla answered a slight smile on her face.

"Sounds like a plan to me." Cody reached for the cutting board and another bowl.

He observed Kayla as she found a couple of tin pie plates, the rolling pin, and assembled the ingredients and spices with the ease of someone who felt comfortable in the kitchen.

They shared the beautiful wooden table as each did their preparations for the pies.

Kayla reminisced of when she saw the table for the first time and remarked to Cody, "I never get over how beautiful this table is. How did you ever manage to get it up here?"

Putting down the knife, he replied, "I made it. Susan and I found this piece of land as our 'get away' and would spend time up here on vacations. When the DNR found out about us spending so much time here, they asked if I'd work for them and do tests, take samples and watch how the animals and Mother Nature worked together. That's why the cabin is so large and has all the extras not found in most cabins around here. They insulated and reinforced the walls, especially the room where all the food is to keep out the critters. They also provided the well for water and piped it into the kitchen." He motioned to the hand pump by the sink.

"The outdoor toilet is specially constructed, but I do keep the commode for the girls at night and when there is a blizzard. I know you noticed the ropes from the house to the small little room with the half-moon door. One can get disorientated and easily lost in a blizzard.

It isn't easily detected that the whole cabin is reinforced. The DNR put metal rods around the house and another layer of logs so it looks like a plain ole cabin. When the shutters are closed over the windows, they are strong enough to resist the powerful bears. That's also why we never throw scraps of food outside. As I mentioned it before, we burn or bury it so we don't attract them.

Beneath the bench by the back door, I have an underground root cellar. I made a stairway so we can enter from the inside of the house too. We get a lot of snow here and it can get difficult to keep the snow cleared to enter from the outside." He paused for a minute as he reached for another apple.

"Did I ever tell you about the wood burning generators they installed in my room? I can use batteries or switch to wood. But it sure takes a lot of time to cut wood and season it. That's why I have such a large wood pile. Different wood burns warmer, longer, and with less smoke. It's very important we keep the wood box full. The weather can change swiftly and it could save our lives."

The sound of Cody sliding the bowl of sliced apples over to Kayla broke her thoughts of what Cody has just revealed.

Stepping over to the stove, Cody poured a cup of coffee from the gray galvanized coffee pot. He sat down and watched as Kayla spooned the apple mixture into the crust.

"Once the snow comes, I should have time to wire up some lights for us to use, but not all the time." Cody took a sip of coffee and continued speaking, "Remember I have that short wave radio in my room, and every so often, they drop batteries for different things. I have flashlights, candle and gas lanterns. We must use all of it sparingly. I use the fireplace when it is extremely cold, otherwise, the cooking range and potbellied stove keeps us pretty comfortable…along with long johns and warm moccasins. I'll make you a pair of moccasins and some leather boots with fur inside. You'll be amazed at how warm and comfortable they are."

Thinking to herself, *he can't be using that many batteries and I never hear him talking on the short wave radio or a plane going overhead. And why all the secrecy of keeping the short wave radio locked in his room? Hum, another thing that wasn't mentioned during the job interview.*

"I'm glad I brought along the warm clothes you suggested, especially my down parka." Kayla remarked as she lowered the heavy oven door and slid in the pies, all three of them.

Turning to Cody she asked, "Do I change the thingamajig now that the pies are in or wait a few minutes."

Cody patiently showed her how to adjust the damper to control the heat in the oven. He hoped she would like the stove more as she used it. It was a beauty. It had a water warming reservoir, the holding shelf on the top to keep things warm or let the bread rise when it was cold in the room, four areas to put wood in and a grill area. It was fantastic, well-made stove and didn't require much work to keep it clean.

During the hot summer, the cooking was done outside on a smaller version in the screened in room.

Cody rubbed his chin. *Um, I wonder if I told her about how nasty the deer flies and mosquitoes can be? But then, her contract is done in the spring.* He thought it might be better to keep that info to himself for the time being.

"If you're okay with the stove, I better get back to hauling wood from the forest. By using the wood from the downed trees, it helps to keep the forest a littler cleaner. I like to cut it in proper lengths up here so I'm closer to the girls.

Did you notice my sturdy little trailer?"

Wiping off the table, Kayla looked up at him. "Yes I did. I suppose you made that too! Light weight on those hard tires with a harness you pull it with." She laughed. "Is there anything you can't make?"

"Not too many things. I'm pretty good at improvising to make or repair items. They might not turn out as good as the Amish make them, but they do the intended job when a Menards or Home Depot isn't around the corner. I was going to get a horse, or dog sled team, but it's too hard to take care of them, and I don't have land cleared for hay and grazing. I love horses, but it's easier to use snow shoes to get around here. There's an extra pair in the storage room you can use."

"Were they Susan's?"

His eyes unexpectantly filled up with grief as he gave Kayla a muffled, "Yes."

Taking his hat off the hook, Cody stepped outside. *When did the hurt go away?*

CHAPTER TWO

Pies And Guns

Soon Kayla heard the sound of wood being chopped. Hopefully he was working off some of the hurt. She noticed Cody had a rhythm as he worked.

She checked on the sleeping twins, pulled the covers over them and went out to take the clothes off the line. She folded them and placed them in the basket. Ironing wasn't a high priority out here. She smoothed things out and hung the shirts and pants on hangers. Maybe when it was colder she would iron since the two heavy irons had to be heated on the stove. Not only had she burned food, no doubt she would scorch the clothes a time or two.

As she carried the basket of clothes into the cabin, both girls came out of their room rubbing their eyes.

"Kayla, we smelled pies. Can we be taste testers now?" Bobbi Jo asked.

"Well, let's peek into the oven and see if they look ready." Kayla replied.

The tops of the crust were golden color. She poked a toothpick in to see if the apples were soft. They were. Picking up a large dish towel, she carefully took the pies out and set them on a board to cool.

The wonderful smell drifted out to Cody who was stacking the wood he had chopped, which quickly brought him into the house. "Can I volunteer to be a taste tester too?" He leaned down and kissed the top of his daughter's heads as he looked over at Kayla.

"What do you think?" Kayla bent down to the girl's level, "Could you use a little help with the taste testing?"

"Yes! We want Daddy to help us." Both girls said as one, which happened often with them.

Looking up at Cody, Kayla smiled, "You heard them, you can be a taste tester too, but wash your hands first so you don't think my pies taste like sawdust."

Kayla nervously cut the hot pie, hoping that this first endeavor of baking in the monster would be a positive one.

"Blow on it first before putting it into your mouth. It's very hot and I don't want you to burn your mouth." Kayla warned all three. Then she took hot water from the reservoir in the stove and made tea for them.

Joining them at the table, she listened to their oohs and ahs as they ate their slice of pie. Kayla took a bite of hers. *Um, this was good. She had passed the apple pie test.* Mentally she patted herself on the back. *The monster didn't win this time.*

***

Cody closed his door, turned and as usual locked it. "Kayla, are you in the middle of something? I'd like to show you how to shoot the guns."

Kayla stopped folding the pile of socks, "Nothing that can't wait. Is it necessary for me to know how to handle the guns? I'm more use to dodging cars in traffic, that's enough excitement for me."

"Yes, it's very necessary. I don't want to alarm you, but just because we are so far away from civilization doesn't mean we are totally safe from dangerous people, and all the wild life. This isn't a petting zoo area where we are protected from them. We're in their territory." He reached up and took a 20/06 rifle and a 12 gauge shotgun off their holders, shells from the cabinet next to the guns and put them in his pocket.

"These two guns and the Winchester 22 are always loaded. Never forget that. For now, they are too high for the girls to reach, but they will be taught to use them later."

"Oh, my gosh! Loaded guns in the house and not even locks on them?" *Was this guy for real?*

"Kayla, out here if you need a gun, you need it now, not after you unlock it, and locate shells, and load it or it may be too late. What are you going to do if I'm unloading a deer and dressing it out over by the tree, and a bear or cougar starts to charge me? Will you cover your eyes hoping I'll turn around and shoo them away, or be ready to shoot if needed? What if I break my leg and you need to hunt for food, or we need protection from some escaped criminals?"

At that Kayla's eyes opened wide. "Escaped criminals? How would we know that?" she whispered in a small voice.

"The short wave radio, remember? Once a day I check in. The ranger for this area keeps me notified of anything unusual. The few people we see will likely be trappers or a ranger, but if Buddy gets his hackles, up, don't ever, ever, let that person in. It could save your life and the girls. I've learned to trust his instincts."

Kayla swallowed and nodded. *She didn't remember reading this in the contract either.*

Cody removed the shells, took off the safety, and proceeded to show her how each of the guns worked, taking the safety off and on, how to clean it, and the use for each one. The 30/06 was for longer range, bigger animals, and the shotgun for shorter ranges like fifty yards. There were different shells depending on what one was hunting. They discussed how far the bullets could go and what they did on contact. Then he showed her how to clean, load, and carry a loaded gun. He also had a sleeve that went over the stock that held shells ready to reload the guns. Then he had her do the same to see if she would handle the guns responsibly.

Bobbie Jo and Beth had stood by the table listening as Cody explained all this to Kayla. They knew they were not allowed to touch the guns until Daddy said they were big enough and had been trained to do so. That was fine with them. Guns made too much noise anyway.

"Time for target practice," Cody announced heading for the door, a gun in each hand. "Kayla, just as the children in town learn not to run into traffic, kids learn about the dangers here too."

Kayla nodded.

Kayla and the girls followed and watched as Cody set up a sheet of paper for target practice on a tree at the edge of the forest.

Cody showed Kayla how to hold the gun against her shoulder and made sure she could see through the sights.

"Now when you pull the trigger, do it slowly and smoothly. There will be a jerk, so hold it real tight against your shoulder."

Kayla rubbed her sweaty hand on her jeans, repositioned the gun and squeezed the trigger. The gun went up in the air, and Kayla went down on the ground with a hard thump. "Ouch!" Kayla rubbed her shoulder.

Cody couldn't help laughing as he reached down to help her up.

Kayla didn't see anything humorous about it.

Still smiling, Cody remarked, "This is an example of what happens when you don't hold the gun firmly against your shoulder. It can pack a hard kick. You also pulled both triggers. Let's try it again, and only pull back on one."

Kayla rubbed her right shoulder. "And men think this is a fun sport," she muttered to herself.

Even though warned, the shotgun caused a recoil, but his time Kayla kept her balance and remained standing.

The target remained untouched.

By the time the lesson was over, Cody said, "I feel confident, Kayla that with more practice, Kayla, you will handle the guns correctly and safely. I'm really proud of you for the strides you've made today. Good job for the first time."

Later he would show her the other guns locked up in his room, but for now she didn't need to know about those weapons, or the reason he had them.

"Well, Kayla, are you ready to go hunting yet?" Cody chuckled.

"Actually it would be something I should do in case I ever have too." Kayla was serious. "It pays to be prepared, and I want to be up to any challenge this wilderness throws at me. At first I was apprehensive, but once I got the feel for the guns, judging distances, knowing how the action worked I actually enjoyed it. I'll admit aiming at a live animal; a charging animal will definitely be a challenge."

"I'm serious too, Kayla. I didn't plan on you getting a bruised shoulder. Sorry about that, I guess I should have stressed more about holding the gun tight against your shoulder."

"Are you ready to help clean a deer next time I bring one home? I still want one more to can since there are some jars left. Um, pouring a jar of venison and gravy over some homemade noodles, makes a great meal. Another month and we can just cut the carcass up, wrap it, and let it freeze in that freezer shed. Besides, it's not all that fun hunting with snowshoes on, and dragging the deer back."

Kayla stopped still in her tracks. "Canning? Homemade noodles? You're kidding, right?"

Throwing back his head, Cody laughed loudly. "You should see the look on your face right now." He patted her arm, "It's much easier than making the pie. You'll be a pro in no time.

Walking back to the house, Kayla, in a thoughtful mood said, "This gives new meaning to the words to 'give thanks for our daily bread'."

CHAPTER THREE

Voice Behind The Door

Jarred awake by the shrill sound of her alarm clock, Kayla rolled over and shut it off with a groan. Oh, her shoulders ached from the kick of the guns yesterday. She lay there trying to remember when her job description went from teacher to Daniel Boone's cousin.

What she wouldn't give for a nice, long, hot shower. Maybe Cody could come up with that next. There was a drain field for the kitchen sink.

Padding over to the dresser, she picked up the ceramic pitcher to get some warm water from the stove reservoir. "I guess there is something nice about Mr. Monster after all," she said to herself as she ladled water into her flower painted container.

Back in her room, she pulled off her pajama top and was shocked to see the huge purple and black bruise on her shoulder. Gingerly touching it, she flexed her arm, no wonder it hurt. She wanted some liniment to remove some of the ache.

Since the air was cool, she quickly cleaned up and got dressed before the goose bumps made her black and blue marks expand.

"Coffee, I need some nice hot not boiled coffee," She said aloud. Just add that to the list of an electric stove, and the electric coffee brewer.

In her warm bedroom slippers Kayla walked toward the wood box to add more wood to the stove. She still hadn't figured out how Cody banked the fire for overnight. When she tried to do it she got such a rip roaring fire going and Cody had to douse the flames.

As she bent over to pick up a couple of pieces of wood, she could hear Cody's angry voice. She inched closer to his door and tried to listen.

"No! I won't risk my daughters and Kayla! I may work for you, but you don't' own me."

"Morning, Kayla, I'm hungry, can we have oatmeal for breakfast?" Bobbi Jo asked rubbing her eyes as she quietly came out of her room.

Startled, Kayla dropped the kindling.

The noise caused Cody to open his door. "What's the matter?"

"I want Kayla to make us oatmeal this morning," Bobbi Jo said to her dad.

"And I lost my balance and dropped the wood," replied Kayla. "Sorry if we woke you up."

Cody looked very intently at Kayla, "No, I was just doing some work. Oatmeal sounds fine to me too. I'll be out to help with the girls in a couple of minutes." He backed into his room and closed the door.

Kayla heard the lock click. Kneeling to pick up the wood, she had many thoughts going through her head: guns, reinforced cabin, like a mini fortress, locked room, and Cody's angry voice. What had she gotten herself into?

***

Cody slammed his right fist into his left palm. *"I wonder how much Kayla heard. Was she eves dropping, trying to hear what I was saying? I can't allow myself to slip up. I better be more careful."*

He paced back and forth trying to decide the best way to deal with the news that they were getting closer. He had to take Kayla out target practicing again today. Her skill in handling the firearms could make the difference between being tortured, killed or used as pawns by the enemy. Maybe he should have let his girls stay with an undercover family, but he couldn't bear to be without them. Losing Susan was one thing, but he couldn't be separated from them at this time. They were too young to have both parents gone, especially with this job; he wasn't able to promise them when or if he would be back.

He heard Beth calling to him, "Daddy, the oatmeal is ready. Kayla said to tell you to 'come and get it or she'll throw it out'. Hurry daddy, I'm hungry."

"Coming, Beth."

Cody glanced around the room. Everything was in place. He came out and locked the door behind him.

Cody turned around and smiled at everyone. "Um, it smells delicious, and I'm hungry as a bear. Kayla didn't throw my portion out did she?" He questioned Beth as he leaned down and kissed the top of her head. Ruffling Bobbi Jo's hair, he took his seat at the head of the table.

The girls giggled and looked at Kayla.

Bobbi Jo pointed her spoon at Kayla, "She didn't burn it or throw it out, Daddy, and it tastes just perfect."

"You sound like Goldilocks in THE THREE BEARS story." He took a spoonful and looked over at Kayla. "This is good Kayla, just right."

Kayla whispered, "Shush, the monster might hear and lunch will be burnt to a crisp."

Taking a drink of his coffee, Cody casually said, "Kayla, I think we should do more target practicing this morning. That's the only way to feel comfortable with the guns."

Rubbing her shoulder, Kayla gave him a rueful smile, "Ah, Sir Hunter, my shoulder is still black and blue."

"My point exactly, holding the gun properly, you can control the recoil, and prevent anymore bruising."

"Okay my Captain, but only after we ladies do the dishes."

The twins looked at each other; they got to help with the dishes again. Kayla was so much fun to have here.

Cody watched Kayla with the girls as the cleaned up after breakfast. He could tell she was swirling questions in her head because she was very quiet. Usually she sang songs with the girls.

Undercover was undercover, but could he take a chance with her life? How much should he reveal to her? He wanted her to be alert, keep an eye out for the unexpected. It was so much easier when Susan was alive. She understood and was his partner in this.

He had about twenty-four hours left before they arrived, unless they changed their direction. Hopefully Hal wouldn't blow his cover and could get a message to headquarters. He sighed. How come James Bond always had so much fun with this type of work?

CHAPTER FOUR

Target Practice And The Truth

Kayla knew Cody wasn't as laid back as he was letting on. Her gut feeling said there was more to it than just another target practice right away this morning. She heard urgency in his voice. Who was he talking to this morning, and why would she, Beth, and Bobbi Jo be in danger? She was going to get some answers out of him when the girls were taking their naps or were out of hearing range.

"Girls, you are such wonderful helpers. We really got dishes done in a hurry." Kayla leaned down and hugged both of the girls. They were so darling.

Straightening up, she coolly asked Cody, "Which gun do I carry?"

"Your choice," he replied.

Kayla reached for the shotgun. "I think I'll go for a wider range shot today. I should be able to hit any target that way. Then I'll go for the rifle, for the longer range. Before we're done today, anything in my sights better be careful."

The last part of the sentence and her tone caused Cody to assess her closely. *Kayla did hear some of his conversation this morning. They needed to talk, soon.*

"Daddy," Bobbi Jo tugged at his shirt, "Can we take our guns and practice too?"

"I thought you said they wouldn't touch the guns until they were older! They're children!" Kayla's eyes were blazing as she spoke.

Cody threw up his hands, "Please, give me a break, Kayla. Beth, Bobbi Jo, go get your guns and show them to Kayla."

The twins skipped to their room returning shortly with wooden guns, no action parts, just the right size for them.

Looking over at a smiling Cody, Kayla acknowledged stiffly, "Sorry, I should have known you wouldn't let them play with something they could get hurt with."

"Apology accepted. Let's go. It's a nice sunshiny day out there." Cody grabbed some more paper for target practice. He wanted to see the sheets riddled with holes in it when Kayla was done with shooting practice for the day.

The twins and Buddy scampered across the clearing, the girls holding their toy guns as they had been instructed. They stopped where they had yesterday, in their safe place.

Advancing to the tree, Cody put up a new sheet of paper. He made a couple of circles on it. Pointing at the target, "The object today is to stay on your feet and make every shot land here, in the center." He walked back to Kayla.

"That's exactly what I had planned on doing." Kayla laughed. Then she took the lead, explaining what steps she was doing with the gun, and then she took her stance, aimed, and hit the edge of the circle. The next shot was in the circle.

Cody and the girls clapped their hands, "Great

shooting, Kayla!"

Kayla bowed and smiled.

After more practice with both guns, Cody hooked up some paper on string. Kayla was going to have a moving target now. He hoped she didn't look at him when she squeezed the trigger.

"Animals don't normally pose and stand still for a shot. I'm going to pull on this string to give you an idea of what a moving target is like. Animals jump, squat low, have different speeds, and have been known to turn and charge. Please, don't look at me. Just follow the target. Shoot when you feel ready."

"Ready," Kayla called out. She watched the paper as Cody pulled it forward, and surprisingly, backward, just as she was ready to squeeze the trigger. She fired. Missed. The next shot was a hit. By the time the paper was unusable, Kayla felt confident she could at least hit a tree and a very slow moving target, like a turtle.

"I'm really amazed at your progress, Kayla. Did you wish on a star to be a good marksman?" Unloading the shells, Cody handed her both guns, reached out for Beth, and swung her onto his shoulders.

"Something like that," she replied slinging the guns behind her and taking a hold of Bobbi Jo's hand.

"Kayla and I are the gun holders," Bobbi Jo announced.

"Yes, we are, Sweetie," Kayla smiled down at the happy girls. "I think when we get back we should play bouncy ball for a while."

"Yes, bouncy ball, bouncy ball, bouncy ball," both girls sang out.

Cody reached up and lifted Beth down from his shoulders. "Sounds like fun, but daddy has to go do his job. I should be back before your rest time."

He looked up at Kayla, "Are you comfortable with putting the guns away? Remember only two shells in each one so we don't damage the spring, and refill the sleeves."

"I learn fast and know the importance of keeping the guns clean and ready...for anything." She looked him straight in the eye.

"When I return, we need to have a serious chat," Cody told her. *Oh yes, she knew something was up, but how much should he reveal? Stick with the DNR story and say escaped criminals were close or tell her the truth.*

"I agree," came her crisp reply.

Cody went to his room and came out with a different rifle, plus a holster with a small handgun around his hips, his nap sack, and a different vest. Putting on his hat, he turned to Kayla. "When you and the girls come in from playing ball, make sure Buddy is in with you. If anything doesn't seem normal and you get frightened for any reason, load the gun and shoot three shots in rapid succession. I won't be out of hearing range of the gun today."

Kayla nodded. She really was scared now!

***

Leaving the house, Cody made ever-widening laps around the cabin and field. He had his moccasins on and was careful not to make any extra noise. He was looking for any unusual signs. The he checked the hill where he had a high-powered field phone hidden that also had a message holder. If Hal was close, there should be information there for him unless his cover was blown.

Climbing over the rocks, leaving no trail, Cody pushed aside some bushes, and backed into a small alcove. Picking up the phone, the red message light flashed. He pushed the on button.

"Should be at your cabin on the seventh. Four total. They say midnight to break in. No witnesses left. I am the only one with a blond beard, wearing buckskin coat, usual hat, so watch your aim. I'll do whatever I can from the rear, but being new, they may make me go first. No further calls."

Cody shut off the phone, slumped back against the tree and checked the time. He had twelve hours. He needed to get back to the house and get ready. He still didn't know how much to reveal to Kayla. When this assignment was over, he was quitting. He was tired of being a target and his girls too. He was also responsible for Kayla.

Peering out and hearing nothing, he retraced his steps to the cabin.

As he was about to enter the clearing, he noticed the grass was trampled down and cigarette butts littered the ground. Kneeling down, he examined the boot prints and counted four different prints. Someone had been here after he made his rounds. He followed the trail of bent twigs and boot prints for a short way. Had there been a change of plans?

Cody was confused. Hal and that group were to come from the east. This trail was from the north. Did he have two different groups coming after him? Hal hadn't mentioned this nor had headquarters. He got a cold chill down his back. Better not waste any time, he needed to get back to the cabin, fast.

At the edge of the forest, Cody paused, wiping the sweat from his brow with his arm when he noticed that the door to the cabin was shut. No sign of Buddy outside. His heart began beating fast, he hoped the date wasn't wrong, or it meant high noon, not midnight. He took a deep breath and then backed into the trees and worked his way around to the out buildings. There was a curtain on the back door that faced the privy. He would see if he could come up that way and hear anything.

Crouching low to blend in with the surroundings, he finally reached the cabin and saw all the shutters were closed. That wasn't a good sign. Cody walked slowly around to the front porch, his constantly surveying the area, and knocked on the door.

"Kayla, it's me, Cody."

The peephole moved, and then he heard the door being unlocked. Kayla's face was pale white. Buddy stood by her side and the gun was within reach.

"I'm so glad you're back. Buddy starting acting different, not like when animals are outside, and I didn't see anything different but I did like you said and I locked up the place. I've plenty of wood in here, the cellar door is locked. The girls' are sleeping. Now, I want to know what is going on! I don't like being left in the dark."

"You're right. It's time to talk." Cody walked over to the girls' room and quietly closed the door.

Walking back to the table he sat down wearily. "I received word that some men I arrested have broken out of jail. They shot a man in the back for his trophy buck. While incarcerated, they made threats of killing me when they were released. One man faked a heart attack, when the jailer went in to check on him, the others jumped him and escaped." Cody hoped she believed his story. "My partner was put in the cell with them and convinced them he had a vendetta against game wardens too. That's how I've been getting my information. His last message said they would be here on the seventh at twelve, and there are four of them. I assumed midnight, but when I got here and saw the cabin shut up, I didn't know what to think. He said anyone with me will be killed too, no witnesses. That's why I was so demanding that you know how to handle a gun. That's not all; I think there is another group of four. I saw signs of four people trampling down some grass by the clearing."

Her face was red with anger as she hissed out at him. "You brought me out here not telling me the whole truth about any of this, jeopardizing my life! How do I know what you're telling me now is the truth? For all I know, you could be fleeing from the law!"

Swiftly, he got out of his chair and knelt by her taking a hold of her hands. "I'm sorry Kayla. I should have been as honest as I could with this, but, when I saw my daughters with you, I was afraid you wouldn't come out here. They were happy and relaxed around you; they weren't with any of the others. I also didn't want to leave them with anyone else. I was afraid they would think I was leaving them like their mommy did. She saved their lives; they don't know how she died," Cody put his head down on his arm.

He was surprised to feel her hand on his shoulder.

"If they were my daughters, I guess I'd do the same thing. I couldn't leave them alone with strangers. At least I had my grandma when my folks were killed." Kayla removed her hand. She did feel safer with him back.

"I'm still angry with you and I don't know if I can shoot a person, but I promise you, I will do anything and everything to protect Beth and Bobbi Jo. Now I know why you made me practice so much. What else do we need to do to be better prepared?" Slightly mollified, Kayla got up and took a sandwich from the warmer of the monster and sat it down in front of Cody. Then she poured him a cup of strong coffee, very strong after being on the stove so long.

Reaching into his jean pocket, he handed her a single key. "This fits the lock on my door. I have the other one. If anything happens to me, take the girls in there and barricade yourselves."

He picked up his plate and walked toward his room, motioning Kayla to follow.

Kayla stood in the doorway as her eyes slowly swept around the room. The only thing normal about it were the bed, dresser, and closet. The desk had radio equipment on it, the generator was there to fuel it, and the rest of the room looked like an arsenal. When did the DNR need this sophisticated equipment to catch poachers and the like? No wonder the room was kept locked!

"Until you came, I slept in your room. I wanted to be there if my daughters needed me. This was my office." He sat down at the short wave. He needed back up.

Kayla didn't say anything. *First he only had one key, now the second one shows up. Then to find boxes, shelves, guns, filling the room...whatever happened to a normal life?*

"Cody, you have enough ammo and guns to fight a war." She left the room with a somber look on her face. This was information she needed to go over in her mind again.

CHAPTER FIVE

The Partner

Hal sat with his back against the tree watching the small fire with its different colored flames dancing in the cool night air. The other men were in their sleeping bag catching forty winks before they headed to the cabin. Little did they know it was less than a mile away.

He thought back how quickly he had convinced them he was what they needed to get to Cody. *Maybe he should retire from this service and be a movie star. Probably win an Oscar.*

It had been arranged that he would be arrested for poaching, and he wanted to get even with the warden, Cody Harris.

Two guards lead a struggling Hal to the cell holding these killers.

"Let go of me, I can walk by myself." Hal tried to move away from them.

Signaling to the door controller, they pushed Hal in,

causing him to stumble against one of his cell mates.

"Whadja do that for you crummy cop?" Hal snarled at the jailer, as he pushed away from the inmates.

All he heard was the sound of the door slamming shut.

Mumbling low but audible to the three men, "I'll get that warden, Cody Harris, if it's the last thing I do! I know the forest around there like the back of my hand; he can't hide long from me" Hal had a menacing look on his face as he took a guarded glance at the three men who sat on the bunk.

Big Jake raised his eyebrow, giving a swift look at his cohorts, thinking, *this was too good to be true. What were the odd of having an angry country bumpkin who could lead them to that Cody feller?*

Leaning forward, Big Jake spoke softly, "Did I hear you have a beef with Warden Cody?"

"What's it to yah?" growled Hal.

"Me and my men had a little run in with him a while back, and we ain't none too happy about sitting here waiting for sentencing. We sure would like to teach him a lesson, wouldn't we boys? That man doesn't own the forest."

"Yeah! Well, unless you're a ghost and float through the walls, nothing's going to happen but we get a day older."

Big Jake snorted, "If there's a will, there's a way, right boys?"

"I've got the will; you guys show me the way." Hal laughed sarcastically. "In case you haven't noticed, the guards talked into a phone to someone else to unlock and lock the door. I don't think you have enough money to bribe anyone to leave it open. By the looks of things, you didn't have enough money for a good lawyer to get you off the rap, whatever it was."

"Maybe you let the señor know there was a little more to it, Si?" Roberto offered.

Hal's stomach churned and he fought to control his emotions. He knew there was more to 'it'. Taking a deep breath to steady himself, "So, you shot a bear and left the cubs to die? Big deal."

The third man who went by the name Frenchy, whispered, "We weren't very good visitors."

That comment solicited quaffs from the other two.

It took all Hal could do to harness his anger and not jump up and start using these men, no not men, animals, as a punching bag. A vision of Susan's face, so battered and slashed she was unrecognizable came to him. He forced himself to remain still. These goons would lead them to their boss. They would get theirs in due time, but for Hal, it couldn't be soon enough.

"If we can get out, would you be our guide to the warden's place?" Big Jake whispered.

Hal snorted, "Well, that will be a cold day in hell, but I can get you there, if you get us out. Cost you though, I don't work cheap and I get first shot at that SOB."

"After I do some carving," Frenchy spoke with a grin, "Then let's see how tough the gringo is."

The sound of footsteps caused the men to cease talking.

"Hey, bearded one, your public defender wants to chat with you. The rest of you don't move, stay where you're at." The guard ordered.

Hal turned and waved to the guys, "Time for my coffee break."

Out of hearing, the officer spoke, "Man, you really played that to the hilt. Do you think the recorder picked it all up?"

"Yeah, I'm glad you came when you did; I was having a hard time not blowing my cover when they mentioned

Susan. I felt sick to my stomach."

The men entered a room, where Hal took a cup of coffee and they sat down and listened to the tape.

"Okay tell me, how do we arrange our escape?" Hal questioned.

"Take off your boot; we need to plant a signal in the heel. That way we will be able to trace you at all times. Now, this is the story you'll tell the creeps. While talking with the lawyer, they let you use the nearest bathroom, which also happens to be used by the police. A jacket was hanging on the back of the door. You check it out and found a set of keys. You helped yourself to them. The Jimmy will be parked outside next to a small Neon and Ford. We also have a signal attached to that.

Tell them you have a friend who is also a guide who has a place in town, where you stow your extra gear, but is currently gone on a job. When you get there, you'll find we put a small hand gun in the lining of your brown leather jacket.

Make your first stop in the woods at the tree phone. There you will find directions to the next one. Make sure you travel around, not go straight there. You need to confuse them. Let Cody know your location when you're close enough to send a message to him. You'll find that at site four."

"Got it. How do we get out of here without anyone getting hurt?" Hal queried.

"It's so simple, I wonder if they will fall for it. If we hear anything suspicious sounding on your wire, the plans for escape will be scrapped.

After you go back, tell them to offer to help with the trays when lunch is served, then put a wad of toilet paper in the lock, so it won't lock. Of course, we control that up here. You use your fork to 'pick' the next lock and find your way out. The lights will be dimmed and the desk cop and the other guard will be turned away watching a football game. The volume will be rather high to cover your footsteps.

Bend down below the counter and head for the side door, which will be unlocked. Then do the vehicle thing. And Hal, be careful, these guys are dangerous and don't give a hoot about killing; anyone, any age."

"Are you going to have rifles and ammo at the apartment? I think it would be better than having those crazies breaking into a store to steal some. But the ammo better be real in case they do shoot at a deer or target. They know guns and that Frenchy character likes to carve. You saw Susan's body."

The men stood and shook hands. They had worked together before, and knew one wrong move and they might never meet again.

Back in the cell, Hal waited until the jailer left. "That lawyer must be fresh out of school. I've got the idiot convinced I'm innocent."

Looking around, Hal pulled the key ring out of his breast pocket and dangled it. "Look what I happened to find."

"Man, what are you into, picking pockets, in jail of all places? Are you nuts?"

"Not like you think." Hal told them about the bathroom and his idea of breaking out.

"Cool man. But I have a lot of 'what ifs'." Big Jake commented. "What happens when they don't hear the door clang shut?"

"Good question, I didn't think of that," Hal answered.

"I know," Roberto entered into the conversation. "When the door gets shut, I'll drop my tin cup. I don't think he will notice there wasn't a louder noise. Keep talking about lousy jail food and how you wanted a big juicy steak. The dumb Americano will never notice." A smile spread across his dark skin. He thought he was so cleaver.

"It's wacky enough to work," Big Jake declared, "If it doesn't," he laughed, "We'll get a second chance."

"This apartment you have, are there guns there?" Big Jake looked at Hal.

"Yeah, my partner and I have our own personal ones and others we let our customers use if they didn't bring one. Usually, they have some big powerful gun that they haven't tried out and lucky if they can hit the broad side of a barn at fifty yards. Lee just stocked us up on things so we're ready to take out another group. We keep a lot of meal packs like the military use. The lighter we travel the better." Hal watched the men's eyes gleam with anticipation of breaking out and start the hunt for Cody.

The men laughed and waited for their dinner to come and a bid for freedom and revenge.

***

Hal, stiff from sitting so long got up to refresh the fire. It was getting colder at night. He was glad he had on his warm brown leather jacket.

As Hal laid some more wood on the fire, Roberto jerked to a sitting position. "My time to watch?"

"Yeah, I can use a few winks. I think when this wood burns down it will be time to go, by the looks of the moon."

Roberto looked at his watch in the flickering light. "How much time to get there?"

"About fifteen minutes. Wake us up at 11:15." Hal spread out his sleeping bag and lay down, prayed, and rested. No way could he sleep. One wrong move and someone would die. He sure hoped his signal and message got through to Cody.

Hal was aroused from his meditation by, Frenchy,

announcing it was time to go.

While the rest rolled up their sleeping bags, Hal stretched, "I need to water a tree," and went into the dark. Looking around to see if anyone had the same idea, he removed a small signal pen from his pocket. He pushed the button three times. It was time the backup men came in.

Making a noisy entrance back to the campsite, Hal noticed the fire was banked, not put out. "Maybe we should put that fire out, we want to shoot the SOB, not burn him out."

"Right," Frenchy added, "At least not until I get my turn at him." He ran his finger over the blade of the hunting knife he was constantly sharpening.

"Let's go, lead the way." Big Jake pointed at Hal.

The full moon gave ghostly shadows to the trees as the men picked their way through the forest.

Hal held up his hand. "Look!"

"What?" Big Jake pushed Hal aside, "I don't see anything."

"I'm positive I saw a flickering light, like someone lighting a cigarette." Hal whispered back. He knew it wasn't any of his backup, because they were behind them and none of them smoked. This wasn't good.

"Yah don't think Ardie thought we left the stash here?" Roberto whispered. "And how would they know how to get here? Think they're trying to move into our territory, Big Jake?"

"Shut up. Let me think." Big Jake took off his hat and scratched his head.

Finally, Big Jake spoke, "Maybe our guide man here, can go over and see who is there."

"Yeah, and maybe I don't want to have my head blown off by whoever is out there. If you think somebody on the other side is your rival, by all means, you check it out. I'm only here to get the warden." Hal was glad it was dark because he was getting nervous. His guys would be behind them, if he was in the middle of two enemy groups, he wouldn't be any help to Cody. He'd better get them all to go check it out.

"You heard the man, we all go,' Big Jake said, "But he leads the way."

"Let's go to the right then and circle the clearing so we can find out if there are others stationed around. No one step on branches or do anything that makes noise. Sound travels in this cool high country" Hal sure hoped his signal was still working from his boot heel and the battery hadn't died. He felt like had a gigantic bull's eye on his back.

CHAPTER SIX

Gun Fire

Buddy padded back and forth, raising his nose and sniffing the air, and then he whined, putting his head by Cody's hand.

"I know boy, something's out there, and it's not good. Let me know when they get closer." Cody patted the dog's head and then ran his hand over his back. He wished he'd had the dog when Susan was still alive. Buddy might have warned her in time for her to shoot an SOS. Cody bent down and gave the big collie a hug.

"I still don't know why we don't hide Bobbi Jo and Beth in the cellar. They would never wake up if we carried them down. I don't want them hurt, Cody."

Cody stood up, "Kayla, I was gone when those creeps broke in and tortured my wife. She had put the girls in the cellar and told them not to come out until I called for them. Can you imagine the fear they were in listening to their mother cry out? I can't put them down there again. That's why it was so important for you to be able to handle a gun, if something like this ever came up again."

"Why didn't you tell me there could be danger when you hired me?" Kayla whispered back, her voice full of anger.

"I didn't think anything of this scale would happen. I'm sorry."

"You're sorry! That's it? You're sorry? I should have been told from the onset that there was a possibility of harm on this job, and about the wild animals! I knew something was wrong when I overheard you say you couldn't put the girls and me in danger."

Taking a deep breath and exhaling, Kayla's voice quivered, "Are we going to be killed?"

The silence was deafening in the dark cabin. Even the fire burning in the monster wasn't crackling.

"I'm scared," Kayla whispered in the dark.

Cody stood up and walked over to her. Putting his arms around her, he gently gave her a hug, and rested his head on hers. "Only a fool wouldn't be frightened. I'm sorry for involving you. I'm so glad you're here to help protect my daughters. Let me check with my captain. My back up men should be in position about now."

Releasing her, Cody went into his room and sent the message, "Your men better be close. I have two groups, one on the north side of the cabin and one on the south. I don't know Hal's location, so I hope his signal is still on." He signed off.

Once more Cody and Buddy check all the peep holes and didn't see any movement, until he noticed a light flicker to the south.

"Kayla, we have people on the south, and more on the north. Someone on the south smokes. I saw butts scattered around this afternoon. On the north side, the grass was trampled down. I don't know if they are the same gang divided to watch both ends of the meadow, or two groups. Hal will have a blond beard and should be wearing a leather coat, Indian leg moccasins, and he always wears a leather cowboy hat with a snake skin band. Please don't shoot him! The government men will be wearing uniforms. Anyone else, go for it."

"You never told me that! How do you know this?" She hissed.

"Buddy told me by his actions that there are people on both sides of the cabin by the way he has paced back and forth."

"I mean what your friend is wearing and now we have all these people around us?"

"Hal's my partner; the rest is part of the work I do, to know things."

Kayla had to move, she was getting jittery sitting there, waiting, waiting for the unknown to happen. Quietly she got up and walked to the peep hole in the shutter. Peering to the left and right, she saw nothing but darkness. No movement, no lights, nada. Closing the hole, she went back to the table where the guns were placed and touched each one, mentally going over how to handle them.

In that moment, Kayla went from feeling like a victim to a fighter. *Who did these criminals think they were to come planning on abusing and killing innocent people? They had another thought coming if they thought they would hurt a hair on Bobbi Jo or Beth's head, not to mention her and Cody's!*

Marching over to the monster she grabbed the pepper shaker and jammed it in her back jean pocket.

Watching her, Cody noticed an immediate difference in Kayla's stance and attitude. Her dander was up. But what in the world was she doing putting the pepper cellar in her back pocket? A rabbit's foot maybe, but pepper?

***

Hal raised his left arm signaling for the men to stop. He could feel cold sweat trickling down his back. He crouched down.

"What's the matter?" Big Jake whispered.

"See the lookout man? Do you know who he is?" Hal pointed at a figure barely visible in the dark, standing with his back against the tree.

The men leaned forward and peered through the dark night at the silhouette of the man holding a rifle. Hal watched as Frenchy poked Big Jake in the arm, "Frankie, that's Frankie, Ardie's right hand man. Want me to slip up there and slit his throat?" Frenchy's crooked teeth showed in the dark as he smiled at the thought of killing the man.

Hal didn't have to strain to hear Big Jake's reply, "Nah, you couldn't get close enough to him with your big feet and all the branches and twigs to step on. He'd mow us down in a minute with that AK-47. I'll use this baby." Big Jake pulled a silencer out of his pocket and attached it to his 9mm Ruger. He raised his arm, aimed carefully, and squeezed the trigger. The almost silent bullet hit Frankie in the temple causing him to slowly slide down the trunk of the tree, collapsing in a heap, making his gun fire repeatedly. The bullets ricocheting off the trees made it sound like an army was in the forest trying to mow them down.

Guns from the other group began spraying bullets in their direction, even though the men couldn't see any targets.

Hal hit the ground and carefully looked around, trying to assess what type of action to take.

The three criminals behind him were like drunken crazy people, returning rapid fire without thinking.

Where's my back up? Hal thought to himself, looking around, hoping to see friendly faces looking back. Slowly he rose, up intent on getting some space between him and the two groups that were volleying bullets at each other.

He took one step to the side, when Frenchy noticed and pointed it out to Big Jake.

Big Jack nodded. No one left without his say so. He pointed his gun and fired at Hal, the bullet hitting him in the back of his left shoulder.

Hal pitched forward from the impact of the shell and fell on the cold hard ground. *Damn, that hurt!* He clenched his jaws tight, not making a sound. He stayed there, not moving, hoping whoever shot him would think he was dead.

CHAPTER SEVEN

Kayla In Action

Kayla jumped as gunfire erupted by the side of the cabin and across the clearing. "Guess this is it." She walked into the office to check on the sleeping girls. Looking down at them, she was amazed how protective she felt. Bending over, she pulled the covers up over their shoulders and gave a silent prayer they wouldn't wake up. Even with all the noise of the gunfire, they didn't move or twitch.

Buddy had padded in by her and looked up at Kayla with an expression she took to mean, 'I'm watching over them too.' Kayla bent down and hugged the collie. She got a lick on the face for her hug.

Looking up, Kayla saw Cody pull four red sticks out of a box.

"I hope those aren't dynamite."

"Flares, I'm going to shoot them off to let the helicopters see the men on the ground. The agents should be near now too. I'm going to open the back door just enough so

I can shoot them off. Get one of the guns and if anyone comes in, fire, don't ask any questions." Cody popped in one of the flares and then opened the door as Kayla picked up the rifle.

Cody shot off two flares when suddenly he fell back into the room, stunned by a hit to his head by the butt of a gun, followed immediately by a long haired, tall person.

Surprised, Kayla clicked the safety off as the stranger said, "Don't even think about it. I can stick you with my knife before you can aim it. Lay it on the table gentle like." The voice talking started to snicker, "Looks like this is my lucky night for carving."

Buddy let out a growl.

"Shut that mutt up before I do!" The intruder snarled.

Kayla moved to touch the dog. "Stay, Buddy, stay." Kayla's voice was calm as she talked to the dog, her eyes never leaving the man with the knife. She didn't give Cody a glance; she only concentrated on the stranger's wild eyes, trying to anticipate what he would do next.

"It's time for some fun." The weird stranger advanced toward Kayla. "Go sit in the chair, I'm going to tie you up. Move it!"

Reaching back to her pocket, Kayla unscrewed the lid from the pepper cellar.

He came closer. "I said move it lady, now!"

Kayla whipped out the cellar and threw pepper in his face.

As he put his hands up to his eyes, Kayla shouted, 'hi yah' and leaped forward kicking the knife out of his hand. With a fluid motion, she whirled around with a kick to his chest, then grabbed his wrist and with a twist, flipped him to the floor.

The coward screamed, "You broke my wrist, you bitch!" He tried to reach for this knife with his left hand.

Once more, Kayla swung into action, sending a kick to his left arm, causing the sharp hunting knife to slide across the floor. The intruder pulled back in fear. She was calling the shots. Picking up one of the guns, she ordered him into the chair. Backing up to the door, she pushed it shut and latched it, her eyes never leaving the cursing man.

She was surprised when she heard Cody's voice. "Give me the gun; I'm only seeing one of everything now. I'll cover you while you tie him up. For the record, the creeps name is Frenchy."

Kayla reached into one of the cupboards and pulled out a roll of duct tape. What a marvelous invention. Grabbing French's left hand, she wrapped the tape twice around his wrist, then took hold of the broken one and with no gentleness, did the same and then proceeded taping his whole body to the chair, all the while he was swearing and telling her he would carve her up like he did the warden's lady when his men came in and he was set free.

The mental image was enough to make Kayla want to puke. She took one more piece of the duct tape and placed it over his mouth. "Now, if you give me anymore trouble, you won't be alive even if your friends ever make it through the door. Do you understand me? You will *never* make it out alive."

"Who are you Kayla?" Cody's voice was full of amazement and admiration, "Kung Fu Kayla, or have you been watching '*Walker, Texas Ranger*' too much? You never mentioned this side of you during our interview!"

"Never mind about me. How's your head?" Kayla was getting a cloth wet for the egg size bump on Cody's head.

"Well, let's just say I have an awful headache, but it beats being dead, which I would have been if you hadn't decided to do your exercises tonight. Thanks." Cody struggled to his feet and sat heavily on the chair.

Outside the shooting had stopped and men's voices could be heard as they dealt with the criminals. There never had been a doubt as who would win, just when.

Buddy went to the front door, his tail wagging in a friendly way. There was a light tapping on the door.

Immediately Kayla tenses up and put the gun in the crook of her arm as she approached the door. She looked back at Cody.

"I bet its Hal. Buddy would be growling, not knowing any of the others."

"Who's there?" Queried Kayla standing to the side of the door.

"Hal, I'm alone. It's over."

Kayla checked the peep hole. With Cody holding his gun, she slid the pole so the door could open.

A man in a bloody leather coat and hat, stumbled into the room, as Kayla quickly secured the door.

"Hey Man, where ya get hit?" Cody reached his friend.

"Ah they shot me in the back, but I wasn't ready to meet my maker yet. Those flares sure lit up the area. The helicopters had those shysters in their sites and it wasn't long and our boys on the ground had them all rounded up except the one occupying your chair there."

Frenchy's eyes were livid. If looks could kill, Hal would be pushing up daisies. It was a good thing the duct tape was firmly in place over French's mouth.

"Matter of fact, how and why is he in here?"

Kayla took over. "Hi, I'm Kayla, the neighborhood nurse. I suggest you sit down over here and take off your jacket and let's see if you have any more blood left to drip on my clean floor."

"Hi, I'm Hal, and are you always this bossy? I've been

shot before and I'll be just fine. I'll get a ride out in the helicopter."

"Glad to meet you, now sit." Kayla ladled some warm water from the reservoir of the monster in a pan and retrieved the first aid box.

Cody eased Hal out of his coat and shirt. He didn't like what he saw. Cody looked up at Kayla and shook his head; put his finger to his lips, indicating she should keep reactions of Hal's condition to herself.

"So Hal, I guess I should tell you the truth, I'm not really a nurse, but I've read about it so just relax and let me play doctor instead." Kayla smiled at him.

"All this fussing, just slap a Band-Aid on it and someone tell me what went on in here. Are the girls okay?"

"They slept through the whole thing. I almost did too." Cody added and told him what had transpired in the cabin.

Kayla, glad for the distraction for Hal, cleaned his wound, applied some antibacterial salve around it, but his shoulder kept bleeding. Not being an expert, she thought the bullet might have gone straight through. She lightly packed some more cotton in each hole and bandaged it. Getting one of Cody's shirts for Hal to wear, she then made a sling for the arm.

Hal's face looked paler now, and that worried Kayla. She gave him a glass of water and ordered him to drink it.

Just then, a voice sounded from outside the front door. "Cody, its Captain Martin. Everything's under control out here."

Cody opened the door to his superior.

"Ah, so here you all are having a party while we do all the work." He looked at Hal, glanced at Frenchy, and then walked over to Hal. "You look like a visit to the doc is in order. Good job done. We couldn't have done it without you."

He gave Hal a handshake and touched his shoulder.

Stepping to the door, he opened it and called out, "I need a couple of strong arms here and a place in the first 'copter out. Hal's been shot. Radio in and let them know your estimated arrival time. There's also a prisoner in here."

Kayla touched Captain Marin's arm, "Ah, he has a broken wrist if there is room on the same helicopter."

Captain Martin looked at Cody with a raised eyebrow. "I'll need a report on this, and that goose egg on your noggin. Want to give it now, or send it in?"

"Perhaps you should have Kung Fu Kayla there write up that report. I was just lying there on the floor watching two of everyone. You might consider having her join our ranks." Cody grinned, "She is one fantastic lady." Admiration shone in his eyes as he smiled at her.

Footsteps on the porch turned the attention back the men needing care. As his teammates put Hal on a board to carry him to the 'copter, his complexion was getting a shade lighter.

Kayla walked over to Frenchy. She leaned down and in a low, menacing voice stated, "If you ever get out of jail, don't ever think of trying to mess with me or mine. I won't be nice next time. Nod your head if you understand me."

Frenchy's head was going up and down like a fishing bobber with a strike on it.

"Good, now you won't slip on your knife and have it land across your throat as you walk out. I'm glad we had this understanding." Kayla straightened up as they came for him. Picking up Frenchy's knife, Kayla asked, "Need some help cutting off the duct tape, Captain Martin?"

French frantically shook his head no! He didn't trust that loco lady.

Soon the sound of the helicopters leaving filled the air.

With Buddy between them, Kayla and Cody watched as the rest of the men on horses rode out of their sight blending into the night.

Dropping his arm around her shoulders, Cody's voice caught as he quietly spoke, "Kayla, I don't have any words to express how your actions tonight saved our lives. If it weren't for you, we would all have been killed! I was just as helpless as Bobbi Jo and Beth. Thank you from the bottom of my heart." Turning he put his other arm around her, hugging her tightly.

Kayla began sobbing.

"It's okay, everything over with now." Cody patted her shoulder.

"But, I was so scared. Then, I knew there was no way he was going to hurt my girls. I would do anything to protect them." Kayla sniffed a few times. "I never knew I could feel that way…able to murder someone if I had to."

"No court in the land would have ever convicted you, nor would the CIA have let it go that far. Some men are just pure evil. Come on, let's go in and have a cup of tea. I think we've both had enough action for one day." Cody took her hand and they stepped back into the cabin. Then he locked the door.

Cody watched Kayla as she got the tea things ready. *What had she said about protecting his daughters? 'No one was going to hurt her girls'? He had many thoughts to mull over.*

CHAPTER EIGHT

Many Thoughts

Kayla closed her bedroom door and quickly got in her nightgown. Opening her door again to let some of the heat from the monster into her room, she noticed for the first time, Cody had left his door open. *Did this mean that all the secrets were out now?*

Kicking off her slippers, she crawled into bed, curled into a ball and waited for the covers to warm up.

In the darkness of the room, Kayla went over the adventure of the evening. She had never been in this type of danger before. During the conflict, she wasn't afraid for herself. Her goal was to keep Beth and Bobbi Jo safe, and of course, Cody. When she took the Judo lessons, the thought was protection and a form of exercise. Kayla never thought she would use it. After all, she was a nice person, and didn't temp trouble by going into unsafe areas.

But tonight she used these skills which came naturally. Never had she felt compelled to hurt another person. Seeing that knife and knowing he would use it with intent to torture and kill all of them, changed her view point. What nagged at the back of her mind were the questions: would she have actually murdered that Frenchy character to protect any of them and what kind of woman was she turning into?

She sighed and her thoughts went to how nice it felt with the warmth of Cody's arms around her after it was all over. Was she reading more into his gratefulness of her help in preventing that madman from killing them? No, there was something else there.

The bed was warm and cozy. Tomorrow she would approach Cody about taking the girls and moving back to her home for the winter. She yawned and fell asleep.

***

Cody took off his boots and flopped down on the bed. He touched his forehead and felt the goose egg was smaller now, although it was still throbbing big time. It wasn't the first time in his line of work that he had been hit in the head. He sighed. He should get up and make out the report while it was fresh in his mind. But, he also needed to have Kayla make out one too. Maybe they could do it together.

Together. Um! Together they made a great team tonight. He shuddered to think what would have happened if she hadn't been there and had the knowledge of Judo. Man, she really amazed him. When he came to and saw two of her in action, he couldn't believe his eyes. What a woman!

Yeah. What a woman. She felt good in his arms too. Was this feeling more than gratitude toward her? Did she feel any different about him?

Cody pulled the home made quilt over him. In that state between being awake and asleep, Cody thought he saw Susan smiling and waving good-bye to him.

***

"Kayla, Kayla, wake up. Bobbi Jo and I are hungry." Beth announced as both girls hopped on the bed.

Brought out of a deep sleep, Kayla raised her arms out of the warm cocoon of the covers, "Burr, my sweeties, get under the covers, its cold in here."

Not needing a second invitation, the giggling twins slipped in, one on each side of Kayla, and snuggled against her.

Kayla put her arms around them and hugged them tightly. How precious they were.

"So, my little munchkins," she gave Bobbi Jo a kiss on the cheek, "How about some nice warm oatmeal to fill your tummies?" And turned and kissed Beth.

From the other room came Cody's voice. "Stay in bed until I get the fire started. In all the confusion, I didn't bank the fire last night. There are a few coals left and it shouldn't take too long to get warm in here."

"Okay, Daddy," the twins said as one. They could hear the sounds of the monster being fed and through the open door saw Cody lighting the old potbellied stove. The two stoves would soon warm up the cabin.

As Cody turned from the stove, he saw Buddy standing by the door. "Hey Buddy. Need to go outside?"

Buddy gave a low whine.

Opening the door, Cody was surprised to see that snow had fallen during the night.

Buddy barked in dog happiness, jumped into it, and made his rounds of the open meadow.

Walking back to Kayla's room, Cody stood by the doorway watching the girls snug in her arms talking up a storm. The only thing missing from the scene was him. Cody shook his head, why did that thought pop into his head?

"Ladies, let me be the first to tell you it snowed last

night. Buddy is out there now, having a ball rolling in it."

Without enthusiasm, Kayla softly inquired, "How much snow?"

Puzzled by her reaction, Cody responded, "Almost a foot! It's early this year. But then Mother Nature has her own time table." Cody smiled.

Bobbi Jo and Beth had bounded to the foot of the bed and Cody bent and hugged them both.

"Can we take our sled out? Can we make a snowman? Can Kayla help us?" Bobbi Jo was excited.

"I think if we clear out, Kayla will get dressed, we'll have breakfast, and then go play in the snow." Cody wrapped a strong arm around each girl and carried them out of the room.

Reluctantly, Kayla left the cozy warm bed and shut the bedroom door. She quickly hopped back into bed. The floor felt like a giant ice cube on her feet. Perhaps she needed pajamas with the feet in them like the twins wore.

Snow! This wasn't good. How could she convince Cody to let her and the girls leave with this much snow? Would it melt, or was it here to stay? She twisted a strand of hair around her finger. In the light of day, did she really want to leave now? Was the danger over? Did Cody feel what she felt last night?

Kayla groaned. *Why couldn't life be a little less complicated?*

Kayla's thoughts were interrupted by a knock on the door. Then it opened enough for Beth to poke her head around it.

"Kayla, you're a sleepy head! Daddy, Kayla went back to bed!"

Cody's boots made staccato sounds on the wooded floor as he swiftly entered Kayla's room. "Are you okay,

Kayla? I know yesterday was a bit traumatic." Concern showed in both his voice and face.

Kayla smiled at him, "Traumatic! Yes. I'd say it was quite traumatic, hectic, and scary, and we need to talk about it. Oh yes, I've been thinking about things, but to be honest, it was just too cold to get up yet. Is the stove hot enough so I can make breakfast?"

"Sure." His face registered relief.

"Then scoot, and this time I will get dressed." Kayla made a wave with her hand.

As the door closed, she quickly pulled of her flannel nightgown, leaving her standing in her white long johns. Putting on warm socks, she quickly pulled on jeans and a heavy sweater. Brushing her long hair, she put it into a ponytail and opened the door.

The air was warmer, and she hurried over to the monster to absorb some heat. "I take back some of my unkind words about you." Kayla spoke to the stove. "Just keep that heat coming."

"Oh, Kayla, you are so funny." Beth laughed. "The stove can't hear you."

Ruffling her hair, Kayla laughed, "You're right Beth. The stove can't hear me or talk back. I'll put the water on to boil and you bring over the oatmeal box for me. You have ears and can hear me." Kayla bent down and hugged the little girl.

CHAPTER NINE

Emotions

Beth and Bobbi Jo gobbled down their oatmeal in record time.

"Now can we go outside and play in the snow? We're done eating, Daddy."

"Then I suggest you brush your teeth and make your beds while Kayla and I finish our morning coffee," Cody replied refilling both Kayla's and his coffee mugs.

"But Daddy, the snow might melt if we don't go out now!" Bobbi Jo said in a pleading voice.

Cody laughed. "My dear daughters, it's too cold to melt right away. You have plenty of time to make those beds."

Holding hands, the two little girls skipped to their room.

Taking a sip of coffee, Cody smiled at Kayla, "Thanks again for your swift action that saved us yesterday. I don't know how to show you how grateful I am." Cody reached across the table and took her hand in his.

Looking Cody in the eyes, Kayla pleaded softly, "Let me take the girls home to my place for the winter. What if there is a repeat visit like last night and we aren't aware of it ahead of time to prepare? I don't think Bobbi Jo and Beth should be placed in that type of danger."

A look of disbelief swept over Cody's face. "You want to take my girls away from me? I thought you understood how I feel about having them close to me!"

"Cody, in the short time I've been here with you, Bobbi Jo, and Beth, I've grown to love them dearly. The thought of them being at the mercy of those killers…I was so frightened last night!" Kayla put her hands over her face and sobbed softly.

Cody moved so quickly from his chair that it almost tipped over as he reached Kayla and put his arms around her shoulders. Straightening up he reached for her hands, pulling her up against his chest. Wrapping his arms around her, he rested his cheek against her head. His voice was husky as he said, "Kayla, I don't want you to go either. You mean way more to me than a teacher and nanny for my daughters. Give me more time here. Please? I can always request a helicopter if you insist on leaving, but my girls stay with me. You were so strong and self-assured last night. You have the same type of strength the early pioneers had. I thought we worked as a team. Don't leave me and my girls."

Cody squeezed her gently, and Kayla returned the hug, her face against his chest.

"Stay, Kayla. Don't go. Please." Cody leaned down and kissed her gently on the lips.

"Bobbi Jo, look! Daddy's kissing Kayla." Beth's voice was happy. "We want a kiss too." The twins ran over to Kayla and their Dad.

Glad for the interruption, Kayla leaned down and

kissed Beth and then Bobbi Jo. She needed some time to digest what she had just heard and felt. This put a whole new twist on leaving.

Holding the youngsters in her arms, Kayla looked up at Cody, "Maybe it's time for the girls to give you a hand clearing the path while I clean up the breakfast dishes."

Grabbing their dad's hands, the girls chorused, "Yeah! Come on, Daddy, let's go out now!" they jumped up and down as only energetic four year-olds can.

"Okay, put on your snowsuits and boots. You will need your warm mittens and hats." Cody said as he reached for his boots, then turned back giving Kayla a very warm smile.

There was a flurry of activity and they were dressed and outside happily making snow angels with Buddy running and barking between the girls, joining in the fun.

Taking her time doing the breakfast chores and putting beans on to cook, Kayla replayed the time she had been out here, especially last night and this morning. She lightly rubbed her finger over her lips, remembering how Cody's kiss felt. She knew he had felt that certain something she felt. Oh, things were going too fast. They needed to talk.

Suddenly the door burst open, "Kayla, come play with us! We made the bestest snow angels!" The snow-covered happy-faced girls said in unison.

"I'm coming. I'm coming! Burr! Shut the door, it's freezing out there!" She smiled and headed for her warm down filled coat and winter boots.

The sun shining on the snow resembled glistening diamonds. The trees were cloaked in a mantle of white. The air was so sharp it almost pinched her nostrils closed. She pulled her blue scarf up over her nose.

Cody had shoveled a path to the main buildings and

swept off the porch. There were also holes where the girls tried to walk, but the snow was too deep for them to move much.

Cody brought the sled around and the girls piled on, and he pulled them over the cleared path to the woodpile. There they loaded some cut logs for the stoves and the three of them pulled the sled back to the cabin, with Buddy jumping in and out of the snow behind them.

Beth and Bobby Jo were having fun, but Kayla thought it was time to go back in and get warm up.

"Hey everyone, how does some hot chocolate and a piece of apple pie sound?" Kayla received a loud, "Yes!" from all of them. Buddy barked.

After they were done eating their pie and the last marshmallow from the hot chocolate, Kayla told the girls, "I think it's time for some lessons now."

"But we want to go outside again, Kayla," Beth replied and Bobbi Jo nodded in agreement.

"But your snowsuits are still drying. You can't go outside in wet clothes. Will you get the construction paper and come over to the table," Kayla said giving the beans a stir.

Kayla sucked in some air as Cody came out of his office with one of his rifles, and locked the door. Even though Kayla was aware of Cody's real occupation, there was still too much danger with the weapons in the room to leave it unlocked. Children moved too fast.

"I'm going to take the snowshoes and check things out to make sure everything is okay. What time is lunch? It sure smells good." Cody looked over at Kayla and smiled.

Looking at the beans and giving them a stir, Kayla replied, "About an hour. I need to make up a batch of cornbread too."

"I won't be late." He leaned over and gave her a kiss

on the cheek.

His watching daughters giggled.

Then Cody was out of the door and Kayla could hear the sounds of him putting on his snowshoes.

She quickly walked over and opened the door. "Cody, be careful."

He waved at her.

Closing the door and leaning against it, her heart skipped a couple of beats. She could get use to those kisses and hearing a family close by enjoying themselves. Kayla shook her head. She better begin thinking a little bit more with her head and less with her heart for a while.

Kayla debated on locking the door with Cody gone. *No, Buddy was here to warn her if anyone approached the cabin.*

Because of the snow, Kayla thought it would be a good time to make paper snowmen with the girls. They made circles for the body, and glued cotton on them. The hats, face and so on were very creative. They became the centerpiece on the table.

Checking the monster, Kayla put in some more wood and began mixing the cornbread. The girls helped using the rubber spatula to put the batter into the buttered pan.

"What wonderful helpers you two are. Thank you." Kayla smiled at them.

The sound of the snowshoes being hung up on the porch wall sent the girls running to the door.

"Daddy's back!"

The door opened, "Yes, your daddy is back and I'm starving. I smell something good." Cody took off his outer ware and hung it up on the hooks by the door. He ruffled their hair and looked over at Kayla with a warm smile on his face. The girls weren't the only ones to be happy to see him.

CHAPTER TEN

Beth Hurts

The mournful wail hung in the cold night air sending goose bumps over Kayla's arms. From the distance came a responding cry.

Kayla pulled the quilts up tighter around her neck and snuggled deeper into them for comfort. The howling of the wolves had awakened her, and she found it unsettling, but why? She was safe inside the cabin. Cody hadn't mentioned anything about wolves. She would add that to the list of things Cody had neglected to tell her.

The vocal wolves didn't sound that far away. Kayla left the warm cocoon of her bed, sliding into her slippers, and wrapped the blue afghan from the foot of the bed around her shoulders and quietly walked into the kitchen.

The moon provided a path of light through the window. Kayla searched the perimeter of the field and forest line for the wolves. Whether they had declared the victory of the hunt, or calling for a companion, they were nowhere to be seen.

Kayla was so intent with the view; she didn't hear Cody come up behind her.

"So, you're the one the wolves were serenading."

Kayla jumped at the sound of his voice, causing the afghan to fall from her shoulders.

They both bent to pick it up, bumping heads.

"Ouch!" Kayla rubbed her head. "First you scare the wits out of me, and then you try to give me a concussion."

"Better add, trying to freeze you, too." Cody said softly as he replaced the afghan around her. He didn't take his arm away from her shoulder.

"I'm surprised to hear them at this time of night. They usually do their hunting at twilight. Or they could just be locating one another. Did you see them? They are really beautiful animals."

Kayla leaned back against Cody's strong chest.

"Do you want to hear about their hunting and eating habits too?" Cody laughed softly.

Just then a howl came faintly from the distance.

"Not tonight. I think our visitor is leaving, and it's time for me to jump back into bed. I hope it's still warm," Kayla quietly remarked, but she didn't make a move to leave.

Cody gave her a light hug. "Let me escort you to your room, my lady." He removed his arm from her shoulder and gave a sweeping bow.

Laughing together they walked to her room where Cody repeated the exaggerated bow again. "Until tomorrow, sleep well, my fair lady." He slowly walked backward with his left arm raised high.

"And to you, Sir Cody." Kayla curtsied.

With a smile on her face, Kayla crawled back under the still warm covers. What a sense of humor he had.

***

Kayla woke up to the soft body of Beth snuggling into her side. "What's the matter, Honey? Can't you sleep?"

"My tummy hurts, Kayla. Can I stay here with you?" Beth's voice was on the verge of crying.

Sleep left Kayla immediately as a motherly instinct in her arose. "Where does it hurt Beth?"

Beth touched the lower right side of her abdomen. "Here, Kayla."

"Did you go poopy yesterday?"

"Yes."

"You didn't slip and fall off the sled when you were playing."

Beth shook her head, no.

Kayla glanced over at her alarm clock. *Three o'clock. Should she take Beth's temperature, make some warm tea, wait and see what an hour brings, or wake up Cody?*

She decided to hold Beth and wait awhile.

"Beth, do you want to stay in bed here with me, or should we go and rock for a while?"

"Will you read me a story?"

"Sure I will. You stay here while I get a flashlight and the rocking chair ready for us." Kayla leaned over and kissed the child on the forehead.

Slipping on her bedroom slippers, Kayla grabbed the green comforter from the quilt holder and went into the kitchen. Placing the rocking chair close to the monster, she arranged the comforter to wrap around them both when they sat down. She then put the flashlight and book on the table by the chair.

Returning to the bedroom, Kayla bent over and took Beth into her arms. "Okay my little one, to the rocking chair we go."

Kayla settled into the chair, with Beth snug on her lap, and wrapped the comforter around them both.

"Beth, what if I tell you a story instead of reading one?"

"Ah, huh." Beth responded as she laid her head against Kayla's shoulder.

"How about 'Snow White and the Seven Dwarfs'?"

Beth nodded her head.

Kayla started the story, but soon Beth's breathing slowed, indicating she was sound asleep. Kayla touched Beth's brow to see if she had a fever. She felt normal. Kayla leaned her head back against the chair and, in minutes, joined Beth in dreamland.

The morning sun woke Cody from his peaceful sleep. He stretched. He thought it was time to get up, let Buddy out and to stoke up both stoves. Putting on his fur lined moccasins and warm robe, he headed for the kitchen.

What a lovely scene greeted him as he stepped into the kitchen. Kayla with her arms around Beth, both of them sound asleep. But why were they there instead of in bed?

Buddy padded over to Cody, then to the door, looking at his master with a sense of urgency in his dark brown eyes.

Cody let Buddy out and went to put wood in the monster. The sound of the metal lid being moved woke Kayla up.

"What time is it?" She whispered to Cody.

"Time to rise and shine. Why are you two out here? I would think the bed would be more comfortable." Cody responded in a low soft voice.

"Beth said she had a tummy ache. I wasn't sure what was causing it and prayed it wasn't her appendix. I wanted to monitor her before I woke you up."

"She wanted to help load the sled with wood yesterday

and she might have done too much. That would have used some of her muscles more than usual. We'll keep an eye on her and see how things go. Thanks for being here for her. I wonder why she didn't come and wake me." Cody said as he knelt down by the chair and touched his little girl's head.

"I don't know, maybe my bed is softer." Kayla smiled at Cody. "I don't mind at all. Isn't she a beautiful child?"

Cody looked up at Kayla, "I'm a lucky man to have two beautiful daughters. Thanks for being so caring." He stood up, leaned over, and kissed her ever so gently on the lips. "And so loving."

CHAPTER ELEVEN

The Phone Call

When Cody went back to his room to get dressed, he noticed the red light on his transmitter was blinking. He sat down at his desk and put in his code.

Hal came on, "About time you started working, ole man. Suppose you're just lollygagging around, sitting by the stove, drinking coffee." He chuckled.

"Since when did you start using a crystal ball?" Cody laughed.

"You know me. I see all, I hear all, and I keep my mouth shut, usually. What I called about is, Thanksgiving isn't too far away. How would you feel about me dropping in with my two nieces and a huge turkey? My sister and brother-in-law won a cruise for two weeks and nominated me, as the favorite and only uncle, to take care of Marla and Janine. If it's all right with you, would you check with Kayla and see if she would mind guests?"

"Just hold a minute buddy. I'm sure it will be okay. It

sure is for me, unless you let some more crooks out of jail." Cody placed the headset down on the desk and hurried out to the kitchen.

"Kayla, Hal is on the phone and would like to come out with his two nieces for Thanksgiving. He said he would bring a huge turkey too. Is it okay with you? I know it would make more work for you, but you know I'll help out doing anything you ask me to." Cody was bobbing his head up and down.

"Is he still on the line?" Kayla responded. "I'd like to talk with him a minute."

"Sure, come on in," Cody lead the march into his room.

Kayla picked up the headset. "Dr. Kayla speaking, how's your shoulder?"

"Fine, Kayla. Getting shot is something we usually try to forgo. By the way, how's your pie dough rolling pin? Cody says you bake delicious apple pies.

The sound of Kayla's happy laughter let Hal know it would be okay to come and bring his nieces.

"By the smile on Cody's face, I'd say he can't wait to see you. Could you bring me a few things besides the turkey?" Kayla asked.

"Sure, the helicopter is a big one. I've paper and pencil ready, what do you need?"

"Just a moment, Hal. Cody would you mind feeding the monster?" Kayla smiled at him.

Then Kayla gave Hal a list of items she could use to make presents for Cody and the twins for Christmas. "I'll pay you when you get here, and Hal, please don't tell Cody what you're bringing for me, and wait till the girls are asleep before you give me the things."

"That's easy enough. I'll just put your things in an

THE PHONE CALL

extra duffle bag and they will think it's my clothes."

Hal paused, "Would it be okay if we came about three days before Thanksgiving?"

"Fine with me," Kayla laughed, "It's not like you have to worry about us being away at a shopping mall."

Hal laughed too. "See you then, can you put Cody back on for a minute?"

Kayla motioned to a watching Cody to come back.

"Your turn, Cody," Kayla handed him the headset and left the room, closing the door behind her. They may be friends, but they were also partners.

"You got me, Hal," Cody leaned back in his chair.

"I thought I would let you know that there isn't a word out there about any drug runs, but we feel uneasy. There is a trapper about five miles from your place that we want to keep an eye on. Maybe you and I could have a look when I arrive." Hal's voice was serious.

"I haven't heard any mechanical sounds out there, and no one in their right mind would travel on snowshoes to transport drugs at this time of year. They would cost too much." Cody said the obvious.

"One of the reasons I want to come early is that the long range weather report predicts another heavy snow fall. They might just do a relay with snowmobiles. They wouldn't expect anyone to be out here or even checking it out. You know how cold it gets after a snow fall." Hal said.

"We can't have another fiasco like before and put Kayla and the girls in danger." Cody commented. "After the last one, she wanted to take the girls and leave."

"Not good. No, we are just going to keep a look out. Do you want me to bring a couple of snowmobiles along, or will we use snowshoes or skis? They have a battery operated one that doesn't make the noise like the gas ones. It could eat up a lot of miles, and we could snowshoe in for the last one."

"You make that decision, Hal. I need to be honest with Kayla. I can't leave her wondering, or in danger, especially with four little girls around."

"Go ahead and tell her. It's not like she is going hear it on the six o'clock news, and yes, someone who is prepared and cautious, doesn't get caught off guard. I'm signing off and should be there in about a week. I'll call if I hear anything, and keep your eyes and ears open. Let's check in at eighteen hundred hours every day until I get there. Take care, Cody."

"You too, Hal. I'm glad you're coming out if it ends up being business or just a good time. I was really worried about your shoulder."

"Hey man, we are CIA, like Superman but we don't fly!" Hal laughed. "Ten-four."

"Ten-four." Cody shut off the transmitter and took off the headset and leaned back into the chair. How was he to tell Kayla that they might be in danger again? Rubbing his forehead, he tried to think of a way to gently bring up the subject without upsetting her. Would she be irritated enough to leave here, leave him? She talked about leaving and wanted to take the girls before. Cody sighed. He didn't realize until right now how much she meant to him. The girls loved her.

He arose from the chair and opened the door, closing and locking it behind him.

Kayla noticed a frown on his face. She went to the monster and poured out a cup of tea and walked over to Cody and handed him the cup.

"For someone who just talked with his best friend, you sure don't look very happy. Want to talk?"

"Yeah." Cody's voice was low and soft. He glanced over at his daughters who were playing with some Barbie dolls.

THE PHONE CALL

"Hal didn't tell me until after he talked with you, but we might have to do some investigating around a trapper's shack while he's here. I think it's a waste of time, and I can't see any drugs moving this way at this time of the year. Another snowstorm is due in here around Thanksgiving, that's why Hal wants to come early. The thing is, while we are gone out on a five mile hike, you would be here alone with the girls. I don't really want to do this to you. You're very special to me, not just as a nanny/teacher for the girls, but as someone I enjoy holding, kissing, and being with. I won't mislead you ever again."

"Thank you, Cody, for being honest with me. I feel better and realize how important your job is to you. I'm okay with life here. You and the girls mean a lot to me too. Don't worry. What say we do a little target practice to refresh my memory, keep extra wood close by, and everything will be okay."

Cody set down his cup and pulled her into his arms. He just held her, feeling her soft hair against his cheek. He felt like they were a team.

With her arms around Cody's waist, Kayla also felt a change between them. A bond was getting stronger. He trusted her with information and with the lives of four little girls. She raised her head.

Cody lowered his and they shared a long kiss. Oh yes, there definitely was a change in their relationship. Good-bye boss verses employee. Hello, Prince Charming and Lady Kayla.

CHAPTER TWELVE

Injured

As the men approached the trees surrounding the weather beaten cabin, they were surprised by the lack of smoke from the rock chimney.

Hal raised his binoculars to his eyes and scanned the surrounding area and cabin. "Cody, I don't see any signs of life anywhere. Even the snow hasn't been cleared off the steps." He handed the field glasses to Cody.

"I think we should still check it out. Back door or front?" Cody asked.

"Back. When I hear you enter the front door, I'll wait until you open the back door. If anything sounds unusual, I'll find a way in. Check through the window before you knock on the door." Hal answered.

"Yes, dad, I'll remember. I'm not a rookie you know."

Both men looked at each other and shared a chuckle. They checked their weapons, and then cautiously made their way through the trees.

Approaching the porch steps, Cody knelt down and removed his snowshoes. The soft snow muffled any sound of his boots on the wood slab floor. Bending down by the window, he slowly raised up enough to peer over the edge.

He could see a body on a bed huddled under a mound of blankets. Cody stepped to the side of the door, reached his arm around to give three rapid knocks.

"Who's there?" A muffled voice responded to the knock.

"Cody Harris, game warden. Is everything okay?"

"No. Come in slowly."

"Coming in," Cody called out as he opened the door and stepped in to see a young man wearing a beard, leaning on his arm with a gun pointed at him.

"Stop right there. Why haven't I seen you around here before if you're the game warden?"

"I've been busy in another section. I can show you my badge." Cody slowly reached for the zipper on his coat.

Just then, Hal knocked on the back door.

"It's okay, that is my friend, another game warden," Cody offered.

"Let him in, but remember, this gun is loaded."

Cody crossed the small cabin with a few strides and let Hal in.

"Our neighbor has a gun so come in slowly," Cody told Hal.

Hal stepped in and glanced around the small cabin. There was a closed door on one side, a twin bed with the young man in it holding the rifle, a small stove, and shelves with various food items on them. A small handmade table with two chairs, and a rocking chair completed the sparse furnishings.

"Howdy," Hal nodded to the young man in the bed.

"We didn't see any chimney smoke and were checking to make sure everything was okay. As cold as it is in here, I guess we made the right call. Any objections if I start a fire?" Hal waited for a response, he didn't want to make the man upset.

The rifle was lowered to the side and the young man nodded. "I could use something warm to drink and some hot water to clean my ankle. Thanks."

"What happened," Cody asked, "that you're in bed with no heat?"

"It's a long story. Would you slice some bread and cheese for me? I haven't eaten in two days! The bread is on the shelf and the cheese is in the insulated chest by the back door."

"Sure thing." Cody went to gather the items while Hal got the fire started, adjusted the damper on the stove and pumped some water into the teakettle and placed that on the stove.

Cody carried the sandwich over to the man. "The water should be hot in a bit...what's your name?"

"Pat. Thanks for the sandwich." Pat groaned as the movement to adjust his position in order to eat caused pain to his ankle.

"By the time you're done inhaling that sandwich, the water should be hot enough for some tea and to take care of that ankle. Do you have any pain medication available?" Cody questioned.

"In the other room there is a box with a big red X on it. All the medical supplies are in it." Pat replied.

Cody opened the door to a colder room and looked around There was a double bed, a small dresser with feminine articles on it. The box was on a shelf by extra bedding and towels. Cody also noticed a woman's bathrobe at the foot of the bed. He picked up the box and closed the door as he exited the room. He placed the box on the table. The room was warming up.

Hal fixed a cup of tea for Pat. "Is it okay if I make some coffee for Cody and me?"

"Yeah. Sure. This tea is so good. I've been so cold, but hurt too much to get up and start the fire after it went out."

In the meantime, Cody had examined the contents of the medical box and found it well equipped. He picked out a bottle of Ibuprofen and shook out two into his hand.

"Take these and then we'll wait about 15 minutes for it to take hold while you drink your tea. Then I'll check out your ankle. I've had training as a medic, so I know what I can and can't do to help you."

Gratefully Pat reached out for the tablets. "Thanks, I really need some relief from this constant pain."

Cody took a closer look at the beard. He was ready to bet the rent it was a fake. But why? He went over to the stove where Hal was replenishing the fire with thicker pieces of wood. Leaning close to Hal, Cody whispered, "Did you get a look at the beard?"

"Yeah, I'd say it would be very good in a play. Did you notice the dirt packed in the barrel of the gun?"

"Yep." Cody turned around, "Pat, the water is ready. Are you?"

Pat nodded and with a grimace and groan of pain, slowly pulled the covers off his leg.

Cody and Hal exchanged glances as the swollen, bloody, bandaged leg appeared.

Hal placed a chair by the bed as Cody poured hot water into a basin and added some soap.

Cody arranged a folded towel under the ankle area to soak up any water.

"Ready?" Cody asked Pat.

"Yes." He was nervous and tense as he observed Cody wipe the scissors off with some alcohol. Then Cody started to cut through the stiff bandage covered with dried blood and was surprised to find the bottom layer wet. He removed it without having to soak any of it.

Cody looked up at Hal. Hal nodded. They both knew Pat needed some professional medical care and soon.

The ankle was very red, swollen down into the foot and up the calf of his leg. There were puncture wounds similar to what a trap would do. Cody wondered if the bone was fractured.

Hal looked at Pat and quietly asked, "Do you want to tell us how this happened and who you really are, Miss Pat?"

"Ow! That hurts!" Pat burst out gripping the bedcovers hard with his hands.

"Sorry, I need to clean out the debris." Cody explained.

"And why did you call me Miss Pat?" He looked up at Hal.

"Because young lady, the beard is a fake, your voice is not consistent as a young male, and the rest of you says 'female'. Your bone structure, skin, eyes, and I'll wager under that hat is long reddish blond hair. So, what's with the disguise?"

"Hal, hand me the peroxide, then the antibiotic cream, and the roll of bandage." Cody interrupted the conversation.

Pat took a deep breath as Cody continued working on the injured ankle.

"Okay. My name is Patricia, but everyone calls me Pat. This is my brother, Ted's cabin. He does trapping. A couple of men came through about a week ago and asked him to guide them over to Fallen Boulder Village. Ted told me to wear this disguise if anyone showed up so they wouldn't take advantage of me."

Pat squirmed as Cody applied the ointment.

She yanked off the beard and picked off the glue remaining on her face. "Ted wanted me to check his traps while he was gone. He said every twenty-four hours, no longer. He does the trap line twice a day so the animals won't suffer. He didn't want me getting caught out there if it got dark before I was done. But then it snowed, and I forgot about where the bear trap was and I stepped on it." Pat started crying. "It hurt so bad I passed out. Lucky for me a bear didn't show up. It took all my strength to release the trap.

Then it started to snow again. I emptied the gun and used it as a make shift cane. I think the cold helped to numb my foot. With my ankle bleeding like it was, I knew I had to get back to the cabin. Animals can smell fresh blood quite a distance. It was the longest half mile I've ever done. At the end I was crawling."

"Owe! That hurts so much." She reached her hand toward the injured leg, tears spilling down her face, and fell back onto the pillow.

"I finally made it into the cabin, put wood in the stove, tore up that dish towel and wrapped it around my foot and crawled into Ted's bed. I thought I was going to die knowing he wouldn't be back for at least a week. Then that heavy snow fell and I knew it would be even longer before Ted returned.

"My right leg hurt terrible, all the way to my foot. I couldn't put any weight on it. I'm so thankful you two showed up." Pat's fear and pain came out with another burst of tears. Her shoulders shook with emotion.

Hal sat down on the side of the bed and put his arms around her. "It's all right now, Pat. We're here and will take care of you. Go ahead and cry. You've been very brave about this whole incident."

Pat leaned her head against his shoulder. She was so grateful to be taken care of, and it was a relief knowing she wouldn't die out here alone.

Cody had finished bandaging the ankle. Then he picked up her leg and moved it to get some motion in it. He wanted to get the blood circulating in the limb.

"It's too late to make it back to my place before night fall. We'll stay here, change the dressing again, make you some warm soup, give you a few more Ibuprofen so you can get some sleep, and we'll take off early in the morning." Cody informed them.

"There is a sled out back that we can use to transport her in. We can make it as comfortable and warm as possible." Hal added.

"Go where? Why? What if my brother comes back and doesn't find me here?" Pat looked like the water works were going to let loose again.

Cody sat on the chair he had removed the basin of water from. "We are going to take you to my cabin. I have Kayla, a teacher/nanny there taking care of my twin daughters. Hal brought his two nieces for a visit. We are going to call for a helicopter to take you to a hospital. You need to get some antibiotics into you. I'm serious when I say I'm afraid you will lose your leg or your life if we don't. We will leave your brother a note and directions to my place. You can write it and we'll put it where he is sure to see it."

Pat was an intelligent young woman who saw the sense in the plan. She was sick of the pain and also knew what would happen if gangrene set in. She couldn't remember what her brother baited the trap with, but it was some kind of meat.

"You said helicopter. I can't afford that. Don't you have a snowmobile we could use instead?" Pat had a frown on her face.

Hal removed his arm from her shoulder and put both hands on her shoulders instead. "Did you forget? We are game wardens and, as such, have transportation available if we deem it necessary. I'm sure our captain will consider this request without hesitation. We not only protect animals, but people too, and looking at you, I can assure him you are a person." Hal grinned at her.

With that, the men went about the tasks of doing what needs doing living in the wilderness without any electricity. They had soup simmering on the stove and kept an eye on Pat as she slept, moaning from time to time. They discussed how they would keep her warm and how fast could they go on snowshoes pulling the sled.

Then they woke her up, "Din, din time sleepy head. Time for some magic elixir called, 'game warden soup', which is ready to eat," Cody announced.

Pat rubbed her eyes. "That better be gourmet soup after waking me up from the first good sleep I've had in two days. It does smell wonderful, and oh, how nice and warm it is in here. I didn't think I'd ever be warm again,"

"Do you want to try and sit up at the table? We will prop your leg on the other chair." Hal asked her. "It might help to strengthen you for the trip tomorrow."

"I'll try," She responded. "You want to give me a hand?"

"No, but I'll give you two arms, pick you up and carry you over to the table. No passing out on me." Hal said. Silently he thought she was a strong person.

Gently Hal put one arm under her legs and another around her waist. She was as light as a feather. He lowered her to the chair and heard the deep intake of breath as her leg came down, causing it to throb. Hal quickly pulled the other chair over and put a pillow on it so she could elevate her leg.

Although weak, Pat finished her whole bowl of soup.

Early the next morning, Cody cleaned the ankle out and noticed some of the swelling had gone down. He repeated the heat packs and put fresh ointment on it, making sure she had some pain relief before he started. Then they had her eat some oatmeal and drink some warm tea. They found a thermos and filled it with hot tea. They cleaned up the breakfast things and had Pat write the note for her brother, Ted.

Outside, Hal put warmed blankets into place on the sled with some pillows. Then after dressing her in warm outer garments, they put her in a sleeping bag and carried her outside and on the sled, covered her up and they were on their way.

They had traveled approximately two miles when they stopped for another rest, and Cody gave Pat some more medication, a sip of warm tea from the thermos and they were off again.

Wearing their snowshoes and pulling a sled kept both men warm. They wanted to get back so they could request the helicopter to fly in that day. Getting medical attention soon was imperative for Pat.

As they approached the cabin, the white smoke curling out of the chimney was a wonderful sight for them.

"Hello the cabin." Cody called out.

The door opened and five heads peered around it.

"Daddy's here!"

"Uncle Hal too."

And Kayla thought, *My man's here, but who's in the sled?*

Buddy was racing around the men as they pulled the sled up to the porch. They proceeded to uncover a sleeping bag. Hal picked it up. Oh, the sleeping bag had a young lady in it! Where did they find a young lady in the wilderness?

"Back in the house children, make room for the men." Kayla gathered the curious children to one side.

Hal gently placed Pat on the couch, and proceeded to remove the sleeping bag. Pat looked at the faces of the children, and Kayla, yes that is what Cody called her. "Hi. I'm Pat." She leaned her head against the back of the couch, totally exhausted from the trip, and her leg hurt from the bouncing of the sled.

"Welcome. I'm Kayla. What can I get or do for you?"

"Pat had her foot caught in a bear trap and needs medical attention right away. Do we have any of those pain pills left?" Cody asked her as he went towards his room. "I'm going to call for the helicopter and see if they can still make it in today." Hal followed him.

The girls all gathered around Pat while Kayla went to the medicine chest to get the medication. Filling a glass of water, she returned and gave Pat two pills.

"I'm so glad to get these, thank you. The men tried to give me a smooth ride, but the leg hurts no matter what." Pat gave a half smile at Kayla even though there was pain showing in her eyes.

"No problem. Is there anything else I can get you? I've supper in the oven. Do you want to lie down on my bed? Can I get you something warm to drink?" Kayla felt sorry for the young girl.

"Kayla, I really need to use the outhouse."

"Oh, you are so in luck. We have a commode we use during the night. It's all clean and ready to use. I think I saw some crutches in the shed. Let me check it out and we can have you able to do your thing much easier." Kayla pulled on her boots and put her coat on.

She returned with a set of crutches and adjusted them to what she thought Pat's armpit would be. Then they headed for the commode, just as the men came out of Cody's room.

"Let us help," both men said in unison.

"Thanks, but this is a women's situation. Be back shortly."

When they returned, the effort showed on Pat's white face. Hal went to her and took the crutches and handed them to Kayla, then proceeded to pick up Pat and carry her to the couch.

"Thank you," Pat whispered into Hal's ear.

Hal sat her down ever so gently on the couch. "We got in touch with the helicopter medics and they will be out here first thing in the morning. They patched us into the hospital and the doctor told us to keep doing what we have been, and they will be ready for you when you arrive."

"Have the pain pills taken effect yet? We really need to redress the ankle, feed you and put you to bed. Tomorrow will be a very long day for you." Cody, the EMT, had a box of supplies under his arm.

"And when that is all done, you can sleep on the couch which makes into a bed, or with me. I do have a couple of girls that come and go in the night, but I think they can all sleep together tonight. Don't you think so girls?" Kayla looked at the young children.

"Yes, Kayla. It will be fun." They all nodded. "Can we watch Daddy fix Pat's foot?" Bobbi Jo asked.

"It doesn't look nice, but you will see what happened if you ever step into a bear trap. You don't have to look, and can go to your room if it bothers you. Pat will make some faces while I'm cleaning her foot because it hurts her when we touch it." Cody explained.

Bobbi Jo went to Pat, "My daddy put a Band-Aid on

my knee when I fell. He makes owies all better."

"Girls, what if we stand out of the way and we can sing our Thanksgiving song for Pat while Cody cleans and bandages her ankle?" Kayla suggested.

The song and EMT Cody finished at the same time.

Kayla observed that Pat's face was flushed. "Are you ready for something to eat, Pat?"

"No, I'm just exhausted and would like to get some sleep. The couch will do just fine."

"May I suggest a least a cup of broth and a sponge bath first. I have a warm flannel nightgown you can wear. By that time, another nice little green pill and, you can visit the land of peaceful dreams."

Pat nodded at Kayla, "I would appreciate that very much."

CHAPTER THIRTEEN

Mystery At The Mine

The whirling sound of the helicopter as it circled the field had the four young girls racing to the window. With noses pressed against the window panes, they watched the snow billow around like a frantic cloud on the ground as the 'copter landed.

Slipping on their jackets, Hal and Cody joined the pilot as he and the two medics left the chopper.

Shouting over the engine noise the pilot stated, "I hope the lady is ready. There's another snow fall with high winds headed this way, and I want to be safely on the ground before it hits."

"No problem," Cody yelled back. All the men quickly headed for the cabin.

On the porch, they stamped the snow off their boots before entering the cabin. The rush of arctic cold air came in with them.

"Time to go, Patricia, but the medic wants to take one look at your foot first." Hal smiled at her.

Her face was pale and frightened as she nodded, and slid her leg out from the warm covers.

One medic took her temp, blood pressure and pulse, as the other checked the bandage on her ankle.

As he prepared to remove the ace bandage, Cody spoke, "I just redressed it about half an hour before you boys arrived."

"Yeah, I think I'll leave it alone. Good job. You've evidently wrapped a few injuries before," the blond haired man with the name of Greg on his coat said looking up at Cody.

"A few. I'm a certified medic."

"Patricia, are you allergic to any pain medication?" Greg asked.

"Not that I'm aware of."

"Then, I'm going to give you a strong drug that will make you very drowsy and keep you more comfortable than you are right now. Is that okay with you?"

Patricia nodded yes. Then she looked over at Hal. "Can you come with me? I'm so afraid and alone." Her eyes pleaded with him.

Hal looked over at Cody and Kayla. "I have my nieces with me while their parents are on vacation, I can't leave them."

Cody and Kayla exchanged looks and Kayla nodded affirmative.

"Hal, Kayla and I can watch the girls until you can get back. The twins need the company of children their age. By that time, Pat's brother should be here and can fly back to be with her. Just call your sister and tell her there's been a change of plans."

"We like it here with Beth and Bobbie Jo, Uncle Hal. We're big girls." Janine took her uncle's hand.

THE CABIN, THE NURSE, LIFE CHANGES

Marla looked over at them, not really caring too much since she was busy petting Buddy. They didn't have a doggy at home.

"We gotta go folks. The weather isn't getting any better," the pilot announced.

Kayla helped Pat put on her coat, scarf, gloves and the men put her on a carry board and got her into the helicopter.

As the whomp, whomp of the helicopter went out of range, Ted emerged from the forest. He had traveled as fast as he could on snowshoes and missed getting there by minutes. He took in some deep breaths. He was frustrated and exhausted. Taking a grip on his pole, he headed for the cabin to find out what happened to his sister.

Buddy padded to the door and whined. Cody looked out of the window. "Looks like Pat's brother is here." He patted Buddy on the head, "Good boy."

Opening the door, Cody stepped out on to the porch. "Ted?"

"Yeah."

"I'm Warden Harris, but call me Cody."

Ted removed his backpack and snowshoes. "I take it my sister just left on the helicopter? What happened? I read the note you left and got here as fast as I could. You left a good trail to follow."

"Come on in and we'll talk. It's freezing out here." Cody opened the door and motioned for Ted to enter.

Taking off his coat, hat and mittens, Ted hung them on the peg. He blew on his hands to warm them as he looked around the room and at the people there. He was surprised to see so many kids.

"Have a seat at the table while I make the introductions," Cody said and proceeded to do so as Kayla poured Ted a large mug of hot coffee.

Then, Cody explained all that had transpired from the time they entered Ted's cabin until Ted came into the clearing, moments after the chopper took off.

Ted hit a fist into his other hand. "It's my entire fault! I was trying to make some extra money to help Pat with the next semester's tuition. That's why I took the guide job. I never should have left her alone! To top it off, those jerks tried to short change me. I never felt comfortable around them."

Cody leaned closer to him and in a low voice asked, "Do you know their names and why they wanted to travel out here at this time of the year?"

"They called themselves Lenny and Carmine, no last names, and they paid me in crisp, new one hundred dollar bills. I hope they are legit ones. They said they wanted to go to Fallen Boulder Village to see if they couldn't make it into a rich man's getaway. You know fishing, hunting, cards, booze, and friendly women. When I asked them why they wanted to go in the winter instead of spring when they could do repairs to the old abandoned cabins or build new ones. They just looked at each other and laughed which basically told me it was none of my business."

"I asked if they wanted to come back with me because I couldn't stay and they said not to worry about them. I left then because I didn't want to leave Pat alone any longer since she wasn't use to the wilderness, and I didn't trust those guys, especially when they suggested I get amnesia about taking them there." Ted took a large swallow of coffee.

Placing a venison roast sandwich in front of him, Kayla said, "See how this tastes while the soup is warming up."

"Thanks, I'm really hungry. To get back here quickly, I've basically existed on dried beef sticks." He made short work of the sandwich and started on the large bowl of rabbit soup with homemade noodles.

No one talked until he finished eating.

Now Cody could question Ted. "These men, can you give me a detailed description? Did they have guns? Any mention how they were going to leave Fallen Boulder Village? No one has lived there in a least twenty years since the mine collapsed."

"They had what I would call the Brooklyn accent, both had dark hair, worn longer, and they were letting their beards grow. Their winter gear was brand new, and they had no sense of direction. I'm sure they need street signs to navigate. Someone has to be coming to get them because there is no way they could even find their way back to my cabin with a map. I just can't figure out why they would be carrying so much money around in the wilderness."

"What about supplies? Did they have extra food, camping gear, any type of phones or short wave radios?" Cody needed more pieces of information.

"Very little, and they didn't have the slightest idea of how to set up a camp or even make a fire. I did all of it and made the meals from their supplies. I think maybe they are going to be picked up by a helicopter since they don't have enough food to be there very long and I don't think they are capable of hunting for food and processing it. It's crazy, man." Ted shook his head.

"I haven't heard any 'copters around here except the one that brought the other game warden in that went with your sister to the hospital. Even snowmobiles can be heard from long distances out here. Even then, they would have to have a source of refueling. Interesting." Cody leaned back in his chair.

Ted yawned. "Can I lay out my bedroll and sack out? I'm exhausted."

At this point, Kayla entered the conversation, "I have the couch all made up. You can sleep there."

"Thank you. Cody, when do you think I'll know about Pat?"

"Hal will call me when he knows something. Don't worry, she is in good hands, and what we did probably saved her leg. I just hope none of the bones were broken, although it didn't feel like it, but I'm sure they will take an x-ray to rule out any fractures." Cody smiled, "Get some sleep; we'll talk more in the morning."

Everyone settled in for the night, and Cody went into his office. Things weren't adding up. He needed to go investigate, but he couldn't leave Kayla alone with the girls, and he really didn't know this Ted either. He finished writing up his notes, got up and locked the outside doors, stoked the stoves, looked in on the kids, and went back to his room. He needed to touch base with headquarters. As Cody was about to shut the door, Buddy padded in long enough for a rub on the head, and then went out by the girl's room. He sniffed and satisfied turned around and lay by their door. He put his head down on his paws. He was on duty.

CHAPTER FOURTEEN

The Hospital

Hal walked down the hall to refresh his cold cup of coffee, his boots making a squeaking sound on the tile floor. Patricia had been in surgery for about an hour and was now in recovery. The surgeon said there was one fractured bone, and they cleaned up the other wounds. The care that Cody had administered made the difference in the amount of infection in the leg. Patricia would be okay with antibiotics and crutches. He refilled his cup and headed back. He wanted to be there when she came out of the anesthesia. She has such a fear of being alone. He wondered about that.

Walking back into her room, he noticed the IV in her left arm giving her antibiotics and pain medications. Hal sat in the chair by her bed and gently rubbed her right arm and hand.

A nurse came in, checked Patricia's stats, smiled at Hal, and quietly walked out, her white shoes not making a sound.

In the nighttime noises of the hospital, Hal reminisced

of when he first met Pat. No, he liked the name Patricia. That's what he would call her. She was a woman, and the name Patricia suited her.

For some unknown reason, she instilled the feeling of protector in him. Yes, Cody had provided medical care for her, but he had done the rest. He remembered how light she was in his arms when he'd carried her to the table for the meal they prepared that day.

Looking over at her face, he thought she was the most beautiful woman he had ever seen. He shook his head. He must be getting loopy from lack of sleep, or all the coffee he had drunk. Why he really didn't know anything about her.

Lacing his fingers through hers, he rested his head back against the chair, and in a couple of breaths, was fast asleep.

The clouds of sleep were fading as Patricia found herself aware of her surroundings. Her left arm felt cold. Glancing over, she saw an IV in it. Her right hand was warm and clasped gently by...turning her head she observed a sleeping Hal.

She smiled. He said he would stay with her. Feeling safe, she closed her eyes and reentered the realm of sleep.

Hal awoke to the sun shining through the blinds just as the morning nurse approached Patricia's bed.

"Good morning. I see by the chart our young lady had a comfortable night." Nurse Kip took in the clasped hands of the couple.

"Yes, ma'am. She was pretty quiet. Matter of fact, I didn't hear anything myself." He glanced at his watch, "Until you came in." Hal rubbed his hand over his stubbly chin.

The booming voice of Dr. Merck preceded the corpulent surgeon as he burst into the room. He definitely wasn't an example for any diet ad, but he was an excellent, well known surgeon.

"Good morning, good morning! How is everyone this fine morning?" The jovial doctor's eyes swept the room, including them all in his greeting. He examined Patricia's cast to see if there was any swelling of her leg.

"Young lady, on a scale of one to ten, what level of pain are you having?"

"About a four, Doctor Merck. But then, I don't know what or when I've been given any pain medication and this is nothing compared to how it hurt back at the cabin."

"You're an extremely lucky lady. The man who first cleaned out the wound did you a great service. Gangrene would have set in, and losing your leg or life would have been the outcome, if you hadn't received that care. You must have a guardian angel working overtime." He smiled at her. "I want to keep you here for the day, and if you feel up to it, I will let you go home this evening. Then if you don't have any problem, I'll see you back in my office in six weeks. The nurse can set up the appointment for you."

Patricia's voice was upset as she spoke, "I don't have any place to go. I'm a college student, and was spending the holidays with my brother in the back country."

"Excuse me, Patricia. My sister and family have a home here in town. I can take you there and we would be close by if need be." Looking at the doctor Hal continued, "My sister and brother-in-law are on a second honeymoon, but will be back after the first of the year. I'm actually watching my two nieces in the meantime."

All eyes were on Patricia. "Are you sure they won't mind, Hal?"

"I wouldn't suggest it if I wasn't." Hal smiled at her. "Besides, you can help entertain the girls. I'm not the greatest when it comes to doing the fingernail polish bit with them."

THE HOSPITAL

Dr. Merck rubbed his hands together, "Sounds like you have a place to stay then, Patricia. I'll be back to see you this evening and barring any unforeseen circumstances, I'll sign your discharge papers." As his large frame exited the room, he waved his hand, "Have a nice day."

"Sir, if you would like to take a stroll for a bit, I'll help Patricia freshen up for the day." Nurse Kip said to Hal.

"Patricia, I'm going to put in a call to Cody, your brother, Ted, and my sister, and let them all know what is going on. Then I'll stock up the refrigerator and get the guest room ready for you. Kip, could you help Patricia order some clothes and whatever else she needs, and have them delivered here? Charge it to my account." He handed a credit card to Patricia.

Knowing that objecting to all of this wouldn't help, and she needed something besides what she wore to the hospital, she quietly said, "Thanks, Hal."

Kip was smiling, "No problem, I like spending someone else's money."

Hal squeezed Patricia's hand, "I'll be back later."

Going back to the house, Hal called Cody and explained the current status concerning Patricia. "I'm going to check with the Captain and see if he will send a helicopter out for the girls and Ted."

"Why not leave the girls here? They are having so much fun with my daughters, and you know Kayla, the more the merrier. As for Ted, let me put him on. Ted, come in here. Hal wants to talk with you." Cody handed him the headset and stepped back to allow him to speak freely.

After talking with Hal, Ted decided to call and talk with Patricia, but he would stay at his cabin and resume his duties.

Returning to the hospital, Hal was pleased to see

Patricia looking more rested. "Hi Kiddo, you're looking good, it must be all that shopping."

"Yes, Sir. They will deliver the clothes this afternoon. I also ordered some make up, I hope you don't mind. Here's your card. I'll reimburse you later."

Hal brushed it off. "I talked with Cody, and they are keeping Marla and Janine there for Beth and Bobbi Jo to play with. Your brother elected not to come at this time since you will be under my watchful eyes. He was going to call you, and my sister said to make you welcome."

"Yes, Ted did call and I understand him not coming in, it would be pretty pricy and besides trapping, he is working on a grant to study wild animal behaviors in the winter." She laughed, "Ted said after talking with Cody, he could trust me in your care, because according to Cody, you are ready for sainthood."

Grinning, Hal remarked, "Well, I wouldn't go that far, but the good Lord and I do have some heart to heart talks every day."

They were interrupted by the arrival of Patricia's lunch tray.

***

Patricia felt a little apprehensive as the black Ford Explorer came to a stop in the driveway of the beautiful home. She would be in a strange house with a man she had only known for a few days.

Hal shut off the vehicle. "Here we are my sister's home sweet home. You're going to like it here." He got out and came around to help her. He handed her the crutches and they slowly made their way into the house.

Once inside, Patricia felt the peacefulness of the charmingly decorated home. She was drawn immediately to the wing back chair by the fireplace. Even though Hal had driven carefully, the minor jostling had her ankle aching.

"Do you want to go to your room, take a tour of the house, or rest in the living room while I bring in your things?"

"That lovely beige chair looks very inviting."

Patricia gave a huge sigh of relief as she handed the crutches to Hal and settled into the chair.

Hal lifted her leg on to the foot stool and put an afghan over her legs. Then he went to retrieve her things and park the Explorer in the garage. Returning to the house, he found Patricia sound asleep.

He placed her medication on the counter and took her packages to the guest room. Then he set about fixing a light supper. It felt good to be off duty. He patted his shoulder holster. Checking the house, he turned on the alarm system, removed the gun and holster, placing them in the drawer by the phone. This was one of the few places where he felt safe.

CHAPTER FIFTEEN

Prison Talk

The sound of the steel door slamming shut sent rivulets of sweat trickling down Carmine's back. He nervously took a seat and lifted the receiver to his ear.

Big Jake squinted at him through the glass barrier, and then reached for the phone.

"So, what's the big news that will make my day? Got me a pardon?" He let out a huge belly laugh.

He watched as Carmine glanced left and right, cleared his throat, and whispered, "I know where your buddy, the one who got you put in here is." Carmine smiled. He knew this would rectify his mistake out in the wilderness with that stupid guide.

Leaning forward, his fat stomach pressed against the counter, Big Jake hissed, "Where? How did you find out?"

Raising his right arm, Carmine wiped the beads of moisture from his forehead. Gosh he hated jails, even as a visitor. Nervously he licked his lips. "At the hospital where I was being treated for my frost bit-toes. I, ah, I saw him go into the room across the hall."

"Yeah, if you wouldn't have gone off halfcocked, that wouldn't have happened to you." Jake frowned at him. *Darn young know it all.* "Go, on."

Carmine looked around and then said, "Well, I heard this loud voiced doctor tell the nurse that Patricia O'Malley in room 302 was being discharged that evening. After the warden and his friend left, I called Lenny and had him come up with flowers for the lady. The receptionist said Miss O'Malley had left and gave him the address!" Carmine's eyes sparkled knowing he'd just made brownie points with Big Jake. Even in jail, Big Jake ran the operation.

Big Jake pursed his fleshy lips and made a tent with his fingers. *Those two bumbling idiots redeemed themselves for stepping out of line with that trip to Fallen Boulder Village. They messed up his plans. But, he still couldn't trust those two modern day Laurel and Hardy boys to ice the warden. He needed one of the older men.* He rubbed his chin as he thought about who to order it done.

Standing behind the concealed window, Warden Sands rocked back on his heels. "Get me the printed transcript of the whole discussion. I'll give Hal and Cody a jingle." *They were right on about monitoring that creep. Let's see who Big Jake tries to contact now for a hit man. We might end up with the whole gang after all.*

***

Hal answered the phone on the first ring; he didn't want Patricia woken up. "Hello."

"Hal, Cody here. Did you get the message about the two city slickers and Big Jake?"

"Yeah. Warden Sands called. I can't believe I slipped up and wasn't alert on that one. What were the odds of

Carmine being at that hospital and on that floor or the doc bellowing out Patricia's name? Jeeze. What do you think our best plan should be? I have to make sure Patricia's leg is okay before I move her, but I don't want her being a possible target either."

"If Warden Sands finds out by the grapevine who Big Jake plans on using as a hit man, we might be able to nip things in the bud. Otherwise, we are sending undercover men to guard your sister's home from the outside. We are using the house behind you and across the street for surveillance. Later today, a delivery truck with the name of 'Hanson's Grocery' will be delivery food to tide you over, two guns, night vision goggles, and ammo. Hopefully you won't need it, but we want you to be prepared. By the way, how is Patricia doing?"

"She is hurting but the pain pills help. She's not a complainer though and doesn't want to be waited on. Last night she loaded the dish washer and washed the pans in the sink while I threw in a load of wash." Hal's voice carried respect for her.

"Are Janine or Marla getting lonesome for their parents?" Hal inquired.

Laughter was Cody's first response. "They are having a ball with my girls. Kayla keeps them occupied and entertained. I don't know how she does it. She never runs out of ideas and the girls are happy just being with her. It was my lucky day when she came to be a nanny for the girls."

"Yeah, and I think their daddy is glad for himself that Kayla is there." Hal chuckled.

"I sure am." Cody's tone of voice changed. "Hal, be careful. You know I'd be there, but I can't leave the kids and Kayla out here alone not knowing what Big Jake may try."

Hal laughed. "I don't know about her being helpless. Kayla did a pretty good number on Frenchy as I recall.

Anyway, it sounds like the captain has enough protection here for us. I'll keep you posted. I don't want you to tell Ted about the dangerous situation we're in, or he might try to come and rescue his sister and throw a monkey wrench into everything."

"I don't think Ted will be showing up, and I'm not in the mood for a five mile snowshoe hike. Talk with you later my friend, take care." With a deep sigh, Cody put down the phone. This was the first time since they were made partners that they weren't working side by side, covering each other's back.

CHAPTER SIXTEEN

Villains Strike Again

Patricia watched as Hal put away all the groceries. Then he opened the flower box and removed the guns and ammo. She caught her breath. *Something wasn't right. First, all the phone calls, hushed conversations on Hal's part, and then that huge delivery of food and weapons and he had just purchased groceries.*

She shifted her weight on the crutches then moved over by Hal. "Would you care to explain all of this to me?" Patricia pointed at the guns and shells. "Why those? I thought we had enough food for the next few days that I need to be here while my leg gets better?"

"Let's go sit by the fire and talk." Hal lightly touched her elbow to guide her into the living room.

Full of apprehension, Patricia sat down at the end of the brown couch as Hal set her crutches to one side.

Stoking the fire, he added a small log before sitting down beside her.

Taking her small right hand into his large one, he looked her straight in the eyes. "Remember the two young greenhorns that hired your brother to take them to Fallen Boulder Village? Well, one was being treated for frost bitten toes on the same floor as you were at the hospital and saw me. They found out where we are and the word is out they are coming after me. At this moment, we are under surveillance by our men and waiting for Big Jake's boys to make a move."

Patricia's face registered fear as he talked. "Who is Big Jake and why would they want to harm you? Maybe we should sneak out to a motel or something; no one would know where we are."

"Big Jake runs drugs and deals with other criminal dealings. Cody and I were instrumental in him going to jail. He's not a happy camper right now. And running away from here would just prolong things and have us constantly looking over our shoulder. I know you are frightened. It's only natural, but I won't let anyone hurt you." Hal slid closer and put his arms around her, drawing her near. "It's best to stay put and be prepared. That allows us to be in control, not them."

With his muscled arms around her, she leaned into his warm chest; the strong beat of his heart was both comforting and exciting. She drew in the scent of his shaving lotion. *Maybe it would be better to stay here.*

Hal gently removed his arms. He had felt her subtle change, the quickening of her breathing. He was positive she was having warm thoughts about him as he did of her. Now wasn't the time to think about that.

Clearing his throat, Hal explained their security plan with the department men watching the house.

Patricia nodded. *She wasn't stupid .Things could get very dangerous, but then, there weren't any promises in life.* Squaring her shoulders, "Tell me what I need to help with, or do in case they would get in or, heaven forbid, you got injured."

Hal's respect for her grew tremendously. "I guess the best thing would be to walk through the house and show you all the security. As for weapons, since you aren't familiar with them, it's best you leave those to me. I don't anticipate us being in the line of fire at all. I also have some mace you can carry if by some chance they get in. Come on, let's take that tour and then have dinner."

***

The black van with darkened windows slowly moved down the street, pausing as the driver leaned out the window looking at the house numbers.

Agent Williams adjusted the telescope, zeroing in on the driver. He snapped the camera, doubting it would reveal anything. The driver had a black winter knit hat on that covered his face with only his eyes and mouth showing.

Answering his cell phone on the first ring, "Lopez, do you recognize him?"

"No. His face is covered, I did see the license plate though and I'm putting a tracer on it, checking to see if the van was reported missing. I think that's our man though. Keep your eyes open. You want to let Hal know?"

"Yeah. Think there's more men in the van?"

"Good possibility, Williams. Just a minute." Lopez quickly went to the southern window and watched the van.

"Hey, Williams. Two guys just came out the side door of the van. Both dressed in black each carrying a small case. I'm letting backup know. You call Hal." The phone clicked off.

Hal felt the phone vibrate and answered. "Company?"

"Right on. Lopez saw two men exiting out of the van, both carrying cases. My guess, guns with silencers. Looks like the driver is staying put. Might want to douse the lights even though the curtains are closed. Back up called. I'm going to slip outside and follow them."

Hal looked over at Patricia. "There are two men out there." He hit the light switch and the house went dark. "Lock yourself in the bathroom so I know where you are."

"I want to be with you," was her whispered response.

"But I'm the target they're after and I don't want you hurt."

"Hal, help me down to the floor and give me that five cell flashlight. I can trip anyone that comes close and hit them with the flashlight." Patricia handed him her crutches.

"I can't let you do that, it's too dangerous. They have guns and won't hesitate to shoot you."

"Hal, we don't have all day and we don't know where they will try to break in." She placed her hand on his arm.'

"Promise me you won't move until I come to help you." Ha assisted her to the floor. "And don't scream unless you need help or they could use you as a shield." He kissed the top of her head and straightened up.

Opening the drawer by the phone, he strapped on the shoulder holster and gun. Picking up the 45 handgun and night vision goggles, he handed her the other pair of goggles and vanished into the night.

Patricia adjusted the night goggles on her head and looked around. Everything had an eerie green tint. At least she would now be able to distinguish if it was Hal or not if anyone came her way. She definitely wouldn't want to hit Hal with her crutch.

She inched her way behind the back of the dark brown leather couch dragging her leg with the heavy cast along the carpet, wishing she had pulled down a pillow to cushion her leg. *This cast sure was a nuisance.*

In the silence of the room, the crackling of the wood burning in the fireplace became magnified, and Patricia strained to hear any unusual sound.

The chine of the grandfather clock in the hallway startled her. She took a deep breath and gripped the five-cell flashlight. *Don't be a scaredy cat. Hal's here in the house.* She peeked around the couch, and then ducked back; expelling the air she had been holding in.

A loud crash, then sounds of fighting came from the back of the house. Beads of sweat formed on her forehead as she strained looking through the night goggles, but saw nothing.

A scratching sound from the front door caught Patricia's attention. *Hal was still at the back of the house with the fighting, so this must be one of the hired killers!* Her mouth went dry as if she had a ball of cotton in it. *Should she try to warn Hal or...*

Patricia didn't hear the door open, but felt the draft of cold winter air sweep across the floor. Then the squishing of rubber boots on the oak wood floor caused her heart to race. She was petrified!

"Freeze! Don't move!" A male voice yelled out.

Patricia cringed as she heard two bullets hit the wall behind her. She put her hand to her mouth stifling a scream.

Someone ran past the couch followed by another man who tackled him. They went down with a grunt, sending a gun flying through the air. As the two men struggled, Patricia crawled over and retrieved the gun. Somehow, she felt safer with the gun in her hand rather than the five-cell flashlight. Her brother had taught her how to handle guns, just not this type. She sat with her back against the wall watching the fight through the night vision goggles. *Which one was the bad guy? They both were dressed in black!*

They bumped into the end table, sending the lamp crashing to the floor. Another punch with a fist to the stomach, followed by a jab to the jaw, and the man with the black ski mask crumpled to the floor with a groan.

"You're under arrest. You have the right to remain silent…"

The light went on as uniformed officers entered the house with drawn guns, just as Hal came rushing into the room, followed by more policemen and another man dressed all in black wearing handcuffs.

Patricia pulled off the goggles as Hal knelt down and put his arms around her.

"Are you okay?" They both asked in unison.

Patricia nodded yes.

Lopez reached down and took the gun from Patricia. "How about me? Anyone going to ask me about my sore jaw? I follow that creep into the house, we trade punches, and you're concerned about the lady with the front row seat." He smiled as he shook his head.

"Better be nice to my lady, Lopez, she can be pretty dangerous with one of these crutches." Hal stood up and looked at Lopez who had blood oozing down his face from a cut above his right eye. "My professional opinion is, I think you might need a couple of stitches there."

Lopez waved his hand, "yeah, all in a night's work."

Officer Williams came into the living room, "Man, Lopez, what's your missus going to say when she sees your face?"

"Let momma kiss your boo boo."

The men laughed.

"The officers have the back of the house secured, and will stay here until a locksmith can be located to take care of the front door. Now, if you would introduce the lady to us, we can all go down to the station together and give the captain a report of our evening's activity." Williams smiled at them like this was just a normal visit.

Hal helped Patricia to her feet. "Gentlemen: Patricia O'Malley, my very brave friend. Patricia," Hal pointed at Lopez, "Officer Lopez, soon to be sporting a black eye, and Officer Williams, a good man to have behind you in a fight. We have worked together many times."

"Gentlemen, I'm pleased to meet you, and I don't think you realize how relieved I am to see you. To say I was frightened is an understatement."

Hal still had his arm around her from assisting her to her feet, now he put his other arm around her and gave her a hug, resting his cheek on the top of her head.

"Ahem, Hal, if you are finished in the hugging department, find the lady a coat, our van is nice and warm and ready to go." Williams smiled, "Since you've been such a help tonight, we'll even give you a ride back." He clapped Hal on the shoulder.

"It's so nice to be appreciated." Hal laughed as he helped Patricia into her coat, and slipped on his jacket, and carefully picking her up, carried her out into the cold night to the waiting van.

CHAPTER SEVENTEEN

Merry Christmas

Kayla stood back and surveyed the tree the girls had decorated with homemade ornaments. She smiled remembering all the fun they all had finding the perfect tree, getting full of snow, and Buddy jumping all over joining in the gaiety.

She carefully placed the presents she had just finished wrapping under the tree. She had stayed up many nights to get all the hand sewing done.

The room still held the aroma of the cookies and pies she and the girls had baked that day. Tomorrow morning she would put the turkey into the monster to slowly roast. Kayla couldn't figure out why Cody wanted such a huge one or all the baked goodies. Sure, Ted was coming over a noon, but even he wouldn't eat that much.

She poured herself a cup of Jasmine tea and settled in the rocking chair next to the monster. She smiled and thought back to the months when she first came here. How she hated that black iron stove to cook on. But, she had tamed it and was now the mistress over it, and no longer used the burn medication daily.

And the adorable twins weren't pupils and girls to teach any longer. She loved them like they were her own. Yes, she had to admit it, and their dad.

Kayla was amazed how gentle and loving Cody was considering the line of work he was in. One would think men in that type of occupation would get hardened and callous dealing with evil people who didn't give a second thought to torture or killing people for hire.

She finished the cup of tea. Her contract as a teacher/nanny was up at the end of May. She didn't know what her future would be, but she sure hoped Cody and the girls would be part of it. She stood up, stretched and yawned. It was already tomorrow, time for some sleep.

***

Christmas morning Kayla woke up to the four girls running from her room to Cody's and back. "Santa's been here! Get up Daddy. Kayla, look at all the presents under the tree!"

Kayla slipped into her robe and slippers. As she came out of her room, Cody with mussed up hair emerged from his buttoning up his shirt. The girls grabbed their hands pulling them both over to the tree.

Kayla's eyes widened. There were more presents under the tree then when she went to bed. She sent Cody a puzzled look.

He smiled back at her.

"Okay my ladies, how do we want to open the presents? Hand out one at a time so we can see who has what or…"

The sound of a helicopter interrupted Cody.

Kayla leaned closer to Cody, "Does that helicopter mean Santa forgot something, or we have a few more mouths to help demolish that huge turkey?"

"Yes." Cody leaned down and kissed her. He didn't need any mistletoe.

Shrugging into his coat and boots Cody said, "You girls watch from the window."

As Cody left the porch, he saw Ted on snowshoes leaving the woods. Good timing, everyone was here at the same time. Cody had a smug look on his face.

The door on the chopper opened and Hal stepped out, turned around and assisted Patricia and carried her over by Cody. "If you will ever so kindly take my lady to the cabin, I've a few things to bring in."

Patricia was transferred to Cody's arms and Hal turned back to get their luggage and more gifts.

"I can take that pretty gal, Cody." Ted slipped off his backpack and reached for his sister. Holding her close, "I've missed you. Are you okay? Are you hurting? Man that cast is heavy." He hugged her close.

"I missed you too. I'm doing fine. Yes my leg hurts, and you're telling me the cast is heavy?" She hugged him back.

"You two get to the cabin where it's warm, and I'll help Hal with that mound of boxes." Cody pointed to the cabin where many faces were watching from the window.

Cody watched the helicopter take off, and then reached for a box, "Did you remember my special purchase?"

"Like I could forget? You only called me ten times a day!" Laughing Hal slipped a small wrapped box into Cody's pocket. "Oh yes, and I remembered the bill too."

As Hal stepped into the cabin, his nieces began jumping up and down, and hugging him with all the gusto that happy children have.

"Hey, my sweetie pies, Santa Claus caught up with us just as we were boarding the copter and gave us these boxes. Do you think we should open them?"

Hal's announcement was met with shouts of, "yes," from everyone. "Okay then, everyone find a place to sit."

Kayla had set out a comforter on the floor and the girl's took places there. The adults took the couch and chairs.

"I'll be Santa's elf and help pass things out if it's okay with you, Hal." Ted offered.

"Thanks. I just happen to have the appropriate hat for you." Hal pulled a green decorated elves' hat from his vest pocket.

Ted put it on and proceeded to dance around causing the cabin to fill with laughter.

"Um, maybe we should pass out the presents from under the tree first and then the ones from the boxes. Mr. Elf, proceed please." It had dawned on Hal that there were many homemade items under the tree and they should be acknowledged first.

The girls ripped off the paper and were happy with the new flannel nightgowns handmade by Kayla. The next gifts were Raggedy Ann dolls. Each doll had the name of one of the girls embroidered on the pocket of the white apron.

Kayla opened a packaged and found the moccasins that Cody had made for her. They all watched as Cody knelt down and put the moccasins on her feet. "I promised you these to keep your feet warm. I also promise you that if you accept this," Cody pulled the wrapped box out of his pocket and handed it to Kayla, "I will love you forever."

Kayla's eyes were misty as she received the box.

"Open it, open it," the girls chanted.

With trembling fingers, she slowly unwrapped the box.

Lifting the velvet cover, she gasp at the most beautiful ring she had ever seen. The round diamond sparkled from its position in the gold setting.

"May I?" Cody asked as he reached for the box.

Kayla nodded.

Taking the box from her, Cody removed the ring and placed it on her finger. "Kayla Egan, I love you so much, I can't imagine life without you. Will you do me the honor of becoming my wife and the mother to my girls?"

Sliding off the chair, Kayla wrapped her arms around Cody. "Yes, I would be proud to be Mrs. Harris, and the mother of two beautiful daughters." They sealed the proposal with a very warm kiss.

Then Kayla opened her arms to Bobbie Jo and Beth. Both girls gathered into Kayla and Cody's arms. "Girls, your daddy just asked me to be his wife and momma to you. What do you think about that?"

The twins looked at each other and nodded their heads up and down. Bobbie Jo spoke for them both, "We asked God for you to be our mommy. He heard our prayer, just like you said, Daddy. God answers prayers."

Kayla smothered both girls with hugs and kisses. "I guess He heard my prayer too, because I always wanted a wonderful man like your dad, and beautiful daughters." She brushed away the happy tears. "This is the best Christmas I've ever had."

Everyone congratulated the happy couple.

Hal felt a tug on his vest. "Yes, Marla. If our love birds could turn their attention towards the tree, we can continue." Hal smiled over at his friends who were basking in the joy of their gift, a new family.

Hall pulled out the first package from the box. "It says here, to Marla."

Marla jumped up and down, "Me, me."

Ted, with a flourish handed her the gift that the young child promptly tore off the paper. There was a stuffed dog, a miniature of Buddy.

Running over to Buddy, Marla told the dog, "Now, I have a doggy just like you, Buddy." She gave the dog a hug around his neck.

Everyone received gifts, which they oohed and ahhed about.

Ted received a group gift of a short wave radio along with the call letters. Now he wouldn't be so isolated from help if needed, and could talk with his sister at times.

The last two gifts Hal took from his coat pocket and went to sit by Patricia. "I know your goal is to become a nurse, and I have no doubt at all that you will make a fantastic one. While you are pursuing this goal, I have this friendship ring," Hal opened the ring box to reveal the soft blue hues of an opal in a delicate gold setting. "That I hope will lead to an engagement ring in the future. The second gift," he handed her the envelope, "pays for the next three years of nursing school. There are no strings attached to the schooling."

Patricia and Ted exchanged glances.

"I will gladly accept the ring. I feel something special for you too, but I can't take the money."

"Patricia, I know there is a ten year difference in our ages. That's why I want you to get your education in three years instead of struggling with a part-time job and money worries. If this bond we are forming gets stronger and we marry, I'll be a very happy man. If, on the other hand, Patricia, as time goes by and we end up going our separate ways, I've contributed a new nurse to the world of medicine. You will then be able to help someone else who is struggling. I plan on taking a desk job in three years; it's time for me to get out of the business of dodging bullets and looking behind me constantly."

"Well Sis, as your big brother, I can't find a problem with Hal's logic. You have my blessing with the friendship ring, and with the kind offer of a paid education." He hugged his sister, and reached to shake Hal's hand. "Thanks, Hal."

"Ted, I have an option for you too. The zoo has an opening that you might be interested in doing research studies on a few of the animals. You could combine it with what you have done out here. It comes with a nice salary, and you could also be closer to Patricia and serve as big brother when I'm not around and, a chaperone when I am."

To everyone's surprise, Ted burst out in tears, and embarrassed, turned around and went out to the porch. Hal followed him. "Ted?"

Ted turned around, "You know how the little girl said God answers prayers? Well, He answered another one today. I've been trying to figure out how to help Patricia more since the folks died, and was wondering what I could do to make extra money for her classes. I prayed for enlightenment on this. Today, God worked through you. I don't know how to say thank you. This is so important to me."

Hal looked at the young man. "What you need to know, Ted, is God works through those who will listen. I've been blessed with a job that pays very well, and I've saved and invested my resources. The scriptures say, to those who receive much, much is required of them. That is what I'm doing, sharing what I have. Let's go back inside before we both freeze to death." Hal clapped the young man on the shoulders.

The rest of the day was joyous, everyone like their gifts and the food turned out perfect. The monster didn't play any jokes and nothing was burned. Of course, the one box from town contained whipping cream for the pies, butter for the biscuits, fresh milk and cream and a drip coffee pot that could be used on the stove. Even Buddy like his snow paw booties, and a large raw-hide bone.

At the end of the day, before they all were ready to retire, they stood together in a circle and thanked God for his gift of Jesus to them. And they all said, "Amen."

CHAPTER EIGHTEEN

The Letter

Patricia reached into the mailbox retrieving the single piece of mail. A white size ten envelope with only her name printed in bold capital letters in a straight line were on it. No address, no stamp, and no return address on it. She turned the envelope over, nothing was on the back. It was blank.

Wearing a puzzled expression, she climbed the stairs to her dorm room before opening the letter. Sitting at her desk, she slid the letter opener across the top of the envelope and removed a single sheet of paper.

MISS O'MALLEY,
THIS IS TO INFORM YOU THAT HAL JOHNSON IN SERVICE OF HIS COUNTRY ON A SECRET MISSION IS REPORTED MISSING. DO NOT SHARE THIS WITH ANYONE.

Patricia reread the short paragraph. *Hal told her he*

would be incommunicado for a while but this.

Subconsciously she twisted the blue opal ring around her finger. *Missing?*

Icy pinpricks of fear filled her. Reaching for the phone, she paused. *Don't share with anyone? Why?*

Picking up the phone, she dialed Cody's cell phone. On the third ring she heard, "Hello?"

"Cody, it's me, Patricia. Can we meet? I need to talk with you right away, it's important."

"Sure. What's up?"

"Meet me by the school library as soon as possible." Patricia's voice was tense.

"Give me fifteen minutes." The phone clicked off. Cody knew by the sound of her voice that something was really troubling Patricia.

It was exactly fourteen minutes by Patricia's watch as Cody's tan van turned the corner and stopped in front of her. Patricia jerked opened the door and slid in. Pulling the envelope from her pocket, she handed it to Cody

Quickly scanning the letter, with a sigh, Cody handed it back to her.

"What does this mean, Cody? Do you know where he was or is? Is this some kind of a hoax or someone's idea of a sick joke?" Her voice rose on the verge of hysteria and she covered her face with her hands and sobbed out, "I'm so worried! I haven't heard from him for six months and now this!"

Unbuckling his seat belt, Cody reached over and put his arms around her. "Patricia, I don't know where Hal is or what he has been doing. Let me nose around and see if I can find out anything. Do you want to come home and stay with us tonight? Kayla and the girls would love to see you."

"No, no. It's just been so unnerving with him gone so

much and now this! Why couldn't he have left the service last year like you did?" She cried into Cody's shoulder.

Cody held her close until she stopped crying and her breathing became quiet. "You know Hal's time table to retire was three years, he wanted to make sure you graduated first. There is only this one year left. Now about this note," Cody tapped it against the steering wheel. "We don't know who sent it, if it's fabricated or not, or why anyone would be this cruel. I'm sure if this information was official, Captain Marlin would have informed Hal's sister immediately and she would have told you."

Patricia nodded. *That made sense.*

"I'll see if there are any rumors floating around. In the meantime, you go back to your classes and act as if nothing is the matter but your next test. Use your cell phone to call me if any other notes show up. Don't open it and we'll see if we can lift any fingerprints from it. Also, don't erase any unusual messages you may receive on your answering machine. If this is a hoax, I want to apprehend the sicko." Cody patted her shoulder.

Pulling a tissue from her pocket, Patricia blew her nose. "Thanks Cody, I guess I over reacted but I haven't heard from him in so long. Tell Kayla and the girls 'Hi' for me."

"Will do. I'll be in touch as soon as I know anything." Cody watched her walk briskly toward the campus building. No one seemed to be observing or following her.

***

Patricia's mind wandered as the voice of the commencement speaker droned on in the background. She had completed her studies and testing and today would receive her RN BSN degree.

She glanced over to see her brother, Ted, friends, Cody, Kayla and twin daughters Bobbie Jo and Beth, Hal's sister Betty and husband David, and their daughters Janine and Marla, all here for her special day.

Tears welled up and trickled gently down her cheeks as she remembered the gift of a debt free education that Hal had given her three years ago at Christmas. How she wished he were here to see the achievement of her goal to become a nurse. She sniffed, *where was he this past year? If he was alive, she was sure he would never miss her graduation, even if he had to come in disguise.*

Applause for the speaker startled Patricia back to the present as the first row of graduates began their walk across the stage to receive their diplomas, and for the nurses, their RN pins.

Patricia dabbed at her eyes, hoping her mascara didn't run leaving her with raccoon eyes. She stood with her row, straightened her shoulders, and as she walked with them, smiled. This was the doorway into her future, the one she and Hal had planned.

CHAPTER NINETEEN

Mr. Jones

For the last three months, Patricia had enjoyed working with the surgical team. She was still in awe of the surgeon's expertise in the field of reconstruction. The positive changes they made for burn victims, children with birth deformities, and accident victims were a miracle to the patients.

Over her face mask, she glanced at Dr. Conrad Deerwater, whose favorite background music of American Indian prayers was playing. More than once, she had witnessed the doctors praying during a difficult procedure. Perhaps that was the reason for the lack of complications with the delicate surgeries they performed. Dr. Deerwater maintained that harmony in the surgery was felt by the patient even though they were completely sedated and that they healed faster.

The staff affectionately referred to him as 'Chief' because of his Indian heritage. He was a quiet, thoughtful man who was never too busy to answer a question, or give comfort to a frightened, hurting patient. He never lost his temper, or acted as if he was 'God the doctor'. She could see why patients and staff loved him.

As usual, Dr. Paul Armstrong was the assisting doctor. They worked well together. Putting in the last of the tiny sutures, Dr. Deerwater looked at everyone in the room. "Well done team. This little lady should be scar free when she is totally healed. Let's put a nice bandage on her head to keep down the swelling."

"Nurse O'Malley, when you're changed out of scrubs I would like to see you in my office. Paul, would you join us too?"

Patricia and Paul exchanged glances. This wasn't a normal request. They both nodded yes.

***

Dr. Deerwater was sitting in a meditative pose as Patricia and Paul approached the open door.

"Come in and close the door please." He motioned for them to be seated.

"What I'm going to say remains inside these four walls." He looked intently at each one. "I received word that we will be receiving a man who is close to expiring. His injuries are so extensive that he may be DOA. He will be known as Mr. Jones. He has type A+ blood and that's all we know until we are told different."

"Mr. Jones should arrive about 1900 hours. I know it is late, but we will operate immediately in room B to stabilize as much as we can. He will go to a private room in ICU. Depending on how the surgery goes, and if he survives, as soon as he can travel, he will be transported to a different location."

"I'm asking you two to travel with him. This may take a minimum of three months. Three months in which your where about will be unknown to others. All your correspondence will be in care of me here at the hospital. You will be safe and I will make all the arrangements. I will also be in and out to access him."

"Chief, is any of this illegal? I can't risk my license to perform an unacceptable or illegal procedure on a mobster." Patricia wasn't comfortable with all of all this secrecy.

"I feel the same, Chief." Paul added.

Dr. Deerwater shook his head slowly, "I thought you knew me well enough to know that I would never jeopardize your careers, nor would I do any medically illegal surgery on any shady characters to give them a new identity. I need to have the most competent medical, single people that I can get. Single because you don't have family that needs you daily. I trust you two to do this and, know you can be ready to leave on short notice."

He got up and walked around his desk and knelt down on one knee to be at eye level to them. "Please, I truly think that with what this man has gone through, we are the only ones that can save him, to make his living worthwhile, not as a cripple, and not so grotesque that he would become a hermit, afraid to be seen."

"Count me in, Chief, that's why I went into nursing, to make a person's life healthy." Patricia smiled at him.

"Me too, Chief." Paul touched the doctor's shoulder, "When do I pack my bag?"

***

"Helicopter landing in three minutes," the voice announced over the loudspeaker.

"Our patient is right on time, 1900 hours as they said. Let's scrub up." Dr. Deerwater said, and swiftly led the way. Side by side, they silently did the required cleaning of their hands and arms. As they finished, another nurse held out the sterile gowns and gloves for them to put on.

"The patient is ready, Dr. Deerwater. The two men that accompanied him here refuse to leave. They are standing there by the door. When I asked them to leave, they said they had permission to be here. Shall I call security?" The nurse was worried.

"No, let them stay, Jean. They have clearance. Everything will be all right. Did those units of blood come down?"

"Yes, Chief."

They broke the beam that opened the OR doors and entered the brightly lit room. The team was assembled and ready to go. Dr. Deerwater stepped over and looked at the MRI results and the other tests.

Jerry, the anesthesiologist looked up at them from his seat on the stool at the head of the patient. "I've got him under lightly; he's really weak so you need to hurry. You better get those prayers going, Chief."

Patricia looked down at the patient and gasped. The man's face looked as though someone had pummeled him with a baseball bat. His nose, cheekbones and forehead were broken. One ear was almost off. She wondered how much brain damage was done.

There was a cast on the right arm, and the left one was bandaged quite extensively. Under the sheet, she could tell the lower right leg was in a cast. It gave her shivers remembering how it felt when her ankle had been broken. Dr. Deerwater was really going to be put to the test today to salvage the man's face.

The soothing music began playing in the background. Dr. Deerwater offered a prayer.

Scanning the faces of those around the table, Dr. Deerwater said, "Ready?"

All heads nodded in the affirmative.

Six long hours later, the last stitch was put in Mr. Jones' face. His face and head were swathed in bandages leaving only room for an airway. All of his nourishment for the next twenty four hours would be through the IV along with his meds. They had used six units of blood.

The man now had a metal plate in his head, his eyes were back in the sockets, the ear was sutured on, his nose reset and had a cast on it, the jaw, and both cheek bones were back in place. The dental work would come later if he survived. Mr. Jones would have one whopping headache when he surfaced from the land of anesthesia.

Patricia couldn't fathom how anyone could do this to another person. She was glad she and Paul had agreed to help him.

The next two weeks went by rather quickly as Paul and Patricia alternated twelve hours on, twelve hours off providing medical care for, Mr. Jones. This was all under the watchful eyes of one or the other of the two men who stood guard at the door. The tall slim one, Harry, and the shorter blond one, James orchestrated who and what went into Mr. Jones' room.

Patricia rose from the chair near the bed as Dr. Deerwater entered the room.

"Good Morning, Patricia. Mr. Jones, today I'm going to remove the bandages. I'm sure that will make you feel better. Patricia, please put the head of the bed up a little higher."

Dr. Deerwater washed his hands at the sink and put on a pair of gloves from the box on the table. Picking up the scissors, "Mr. Jones, I'm going to start cutting through the layers of bandages. It will be easier on you than I unwrapped them. Please don't move. Can you hear me and understand?"

Mr. Jones nodded ever so slightly.

"Patricia, please close the blinds and turn down the light before we uncover his eyes."

"Very good. I'm starting now." Carefully Dr. Deerwater cut through the layers of gauze and removed them.

It was almost miraculous how much the man's face had healed. Patricia looked at Dr. Deerwater with astonishment.

He shook his head no and pointed his right finger up. "That is the work of the healer."

"Mr. Jones, keep your eyes closed until I ask you to open them." Slowly Dr. Deerwater removed the pads. Gently he bathed the eyes with sterile water.

"Whenever you are ready, Mr. Jones, open your eyes." The doctor said quietly, hoping and praying the man could see.

Patricia and the Chief watched very intently as Mr. Jones eyelids fluttered a couple of times, and then stayed open.

The doctor waited about thirty seconds for the eyes to adjust. "What do you see, Mr. Jones?"

A soft hoarse reply, "A man," as a tear slowly trickled down his face.

CHAPTER TWENTY

The Lodge

Patricia kept her hand on Mr. Jones' arm as the helicopter landed on the crushed rock driveway, as close to the large log cabin hunting lodge as possible. *So this is Dr. Deerwater's little cabin in the woods.* She smiled to herself. *Some little cabin! It looks like a small resort.*

Harry, James, Paul and the pilot carried the patient out of the copter and to the porch, where the small staff of two were waiting on the porch that surrounded the front and side of the lodge. There they put the legs down on the gurney.

The woman stepped forward, "Hello, I'm Sierra, housekeeper and cook." Touching the man's arm, "this is my husband Joe. Dr. Deerwater is my cousin. I will show you where to take Mr. Jones." She turned around causing her long thick black braid to swing across her back. Sierra was dressed in a long brown cotton skirt that touched the top of her beaded moccasins. A bright red blouse belted at the waist with a green scarf, completed her outfit.

The pilot and Joe went back to the helicopter for the luggage and supplies.

Patricia followed the men and the gurney into the great room and stopped to appreciate the beauty and serenity of the room. She was immediately drawn to the large stone fireplace with a painted picture of Dr. Deerwater. The top of the mantle held some unique pottery.

There were two couches with carved wooden arms and backs that faced each other with a coffee table made from pieces of wood and medium size branches shaped and varnished between them. Bright colored Indian blankets were thrown over the backs of the furniture. Hand woven rugs were scattered across the highly polished wood floor and under the coffee table.

On the north side of the room, was a grand piano and many drums of various sizes on the floor around it. A large sliding glass door to the porch gave one an awesome view.

Comfortable chairs were scattered around the room with some interesting shaped handmade tables similar to the one by the couches next to them.

The wall behind the piano held bookshelves from ceiling to floor with a sliding ladder like the libraries have to procure a book from the high places.

The signed pictures on the wall all depicted Indians in various activities. Such talent this room held.

Patricia noticed she was alone and hurried to catch up with the others.

Sierra stopped, stood to one side and gestured at the open doorway. "Our guest will stay in this room." She inclined her head toward Patricia, "Your room is to the left and yours sir," she pointed to Paul, "is to the right. There are adjoining doors, so you may each assist Mr. Jones at any time. Across the hall is the surgery room if you need any supplies or medication. Here is the key. Please mark down any medications you use on the form on the clipboard at the desk."

Pointing next to the surgery, "These two rooms are for the gentlemen in your party. There is an intercom here by the door to reach me. The numbers are the different rooms. 'K' is for kitchen etc. While you are getting Mr. Jones settled into his bed, I will get some nourishment ready for all of you." With that, she quietly went down the hall.

"I think Mr. Jones will feel better when we get him transferred to this hospital bed." Patricia was folding down the sheet and light weight blanket.

Patricia, Paul, Joe and Harry taking a hold of the bottom sheet on the gurney, lifted Mr. Jones to the bed. He groaned as they moved him.

As they finished getting him settled, Patricia hung the IV bag on the pole, "I'm sorry that caused you so much discomfort, Mr. Jones. That pain medication needs a little booster."

Paul set the insulated bag up on the table and retrieved the needed medication. He inserted the needle into the bottle, drew out the prescribed amount, cleaned off the opening and released the medication into the IV. "That will give you some relief in a minute. Can I do anything else for you?"

Exhausted, Mr. Jones slowly shook his head no.

"Then I think it's a good idea for you to sleep if you can. If you do need anything, I'll be right here in the chair." Paul patted the man's shoulder.

"Paul, if it's all right with you, I think I'll take a look at the layout of the house and then put my things away."

"Go ahead, I'll chart the injection and set up the medications and supplies on the counter and refrigerator." Paul smiled at her.

As Patricia reached the doorway she saw Harry

carrying her suitcases to her room.

"Thanks Harry."

"No problem, Patricia. James and I are right across the hall as you know and will be in and out patrolling the area at different times. Just call if you need us."

Walking in the direction of the kitchen, she thought about the two men that were here as bodyguards to Mr. Jones. *Who was he? What did he do and why would he need bodyguards? She was sure the Chief knew something about it, but he was very taciturn and would never reveal anything confidential, unless he didn't know either.*

Patricia was surprised to find that the kitchen was very modern with stainless steel appliances, and large enough to cook for a crowd. A huge wooden legged table with carved symbols was in the middle of the room and could easily sit twenty people. To the left of the kitchen door was a walk-in cooler and freezer.

The room, decorated as though it was Sierra's very own home, had hand sewed yellow curtains with tiebacks on the windows. Small clay pots on the window sills held herbs that Sierra used in her cooking.

On a round table near a window was a large sun tea jug on a tray with glasses round it. The same person who made the tables in the great room must have made this one too.

As she surveyed the kitchen, the aroma of something cooking made her mouth water. "Um, that smells wonderful. I hope it's on the menu for tonight." Patricia smiled at Sierra.

"Yes, Ma'am. I do have some banana bread and tea for a small snack until dinner. Will that be sufficient?" Sierra wiped her hands on a towel.

"Oh yes, the bread and tea will be appreciated. And please, call me Patricia. You must enjoy working in such a lovely kitchen. It feels so comfortable in here. Do you have help when the doctor is here with a lot of friends or patients?"

"Not usually. If I need to, there are many cousins to call on to assist me. Most of the time there are only four or five extra here. Some famous people like to recover without any press around." Sierra smiled, "At first they don't eat much so I make a lot of soup, puddings and juices. Later, with the walks and exercising, they like foods they can chew. If you have any requests for certain foods, please let me know."

Joe came in the back door and nodded to the women. "I will be gone for a couple of hours. The men want to look around the property."

"Thanks for telling me, dinner will be ready by then." Sierra and Joe exchanged warm smiles and Joe left closing the door behind him.

"He is a good man." Sierra said as she handed Patricia a tray with the tea things on it.

CHAPTER TWENTY-ONE

First Day Of Recovery

Patricia awoke to a faint sound of chanting. Slipping out of bed, she went to her open window that faced the east. There in the stillness of the early morning with the sun almost ready to rise over the mountain, she could hear it again.

"Ajahjah, ajayaha, Spirit of the sun we welcome you. May your rays fill our day with goodness. We thank you for keeping away bad spirits of the night. Ajahjah, ah ah. Spirit fill the earth with your blessing. Ajaha, ajaha."

Putting on her robe and slippers, she quietly nodded at James, who from his room, kept an eye on Mr. Jones' door. She went out the back door, stopping on the porch and listened to the morning prayer. She surmised that the cabin belonged to Sierra and her husband Joe. It must be Joe chanting his morning prayers.

Sitting down on the rocking chair, she bowed her head and offered up her own prayers and for all those around her and especially for Mr. Jones and Hal, wherever he was.

FIRST DAY OF RECOVERY

She leaned her head back and closed her eyes, listening to the birds chirping and the different sounds of the early morning that filled the air around her. She felt at peace.

Soft footsteps came up behind her and then hands gently massaged her shoulders, "Good morning, Patricia. I trust you slept well."

"Good morning, Paul, I did, thank you. How did Mr. Jones do during the night?"

"He did much better. His pain wasn't so bad, and he only woke up twice and went right back to sleep after his medication. Of course, he isn't a complainer either. I'll give him his morning bath and then you can take over and I'll take my run and get some shuteye."

"Perhaps, Dr. Paul, you would like some breakfast first." Sierra said softly as she opened the screen startling them both.

"I think I will wait until later," Paul smiled at her. "I better go back to Mr. Jones."

"And I need to take a shower and get dressed." Patricia rose and left the room. She wondered what Sierra though of Paul massaging her shoulders. It was just a friendly gesture that they all did to one another, especially after a long surgery.

***

"Good morning, Mr. Jones. It is a beautiful morning here in this lovely country. Paul tells me you had a good night, not as much pain. Would you like some oatmeal or a poached egg for breakfast? Sierra is already in the kitchen." A few still damp pieces of hair curled around her smiling face.

In his soft hoarse voice he replied, "I'm not really hungry. Could you call me Reid instead of Mr. Jones?" He looked at her, so beautiful without all the makeup most young ladies wore. It wasn't needed out here, wherever here was.

This was good news, he remembers his first name. "Of

course, Reid, no one was told your first name. I like it, very masculine, it fits you. As for not feeling hungry, I know that pain medication sometimes affects the appetite. I'll put the head of the bed up a little higher and with you sitting up more, perhaps that will help. Later today, we will help you get in the wheel chair and go out on the porch. It is so lovely out there. For now, I'll get you a bowl of oatmeal and some juice. Would you like some coffee or tea with that?"

"Coffee, black please." Reid smiled at her, the stitches still healing on his new face. "You were right; sitting up is better; putting the pillow under the arm helps support that cast too. Thank you."

"Hey, that's what I'm here for, to make you feel comfortable and get well. I'll get that breakfast tray now."

Patricia stopped at the door and touched James on the shoulder, "James, my man, how about a tray for you too or is Harry coming on soon and you can enjoy Sierra's kitchen?"

"Thanks, but I'll eat later, then I can visit with Joe a bit. This so-called cabin is on a lot of land and Joe was raised around here, so it's very interesting to talk with him. While you're gone, I'll keep an eye on Reid so he doesn't get up and start dancing."

"You do that." Patricia laughed and headed down the hall towards the kitchen where she found Harry and Joe talking and eating. They had a map on the table between them.

"Good morning gentlemen. I hope you left some breakfast for the rest of us." Patricia said as she headed for the coffee pot and helped herself to a cup of coffee and a generous amount of vanilla flavored coffee creamer. "Um, nothing like that first cup of coffee."

"What would you like for Mr. Jones this morning?" Sierra asked.

"He said he wasn't hungry, but I think we will go with

some of that oatmeal you have there and a glass of juice. He also requested coffee, black. Oh, and he asked to be called Reid." Patricia put a little honey on top of the oatmeal, and milk into a glass. She fixed the same for herself and added a bran muffin and a pat of butter to the tray. "I think it is a good sign that he even asked for coffee."

"Let me carry that tray for you, Patricia." Harry said as he rose from the chair. "Thank you, Sierra, for a delicious breakfast, and for the information, Joe." He picked up the tray and followed Patricia to Reid's room.

"About time you showed up, Harry. I suppose you ate every last thing in the kitchen." James joked as he got up from his chair.

"No, but you better hurry. I saw Paul coming back from his morning run and I know that young man has a huge appetite." Harry placed the tray down on the counter, and walked back by James. Quietly he said, "When you get done with breakfast, I'll share the talk I had with Joe. Look over the map on the table while you eat."

Transferring Reid's meal to the bed table, Patricia asked, "Are you right or left handed, Reid?"

"Left."

"Do you want to try and feed yourself, or would you like me to assist you?" Patricia asked as she arranged a cloth napkin across his chest to catch any food that might not make it all the way to Reid's mouth.

"I'll try." Reid managed two spoonfuls and put down the spoon, exhausted. He looked up at Patricia, "I've had enough."

"What if I help you with a few more bites? You need to keep your strength up and then we can get rid of that IV in your arm. I know it's hard with a cast on one arm and the IV in the other."

THE CABIN, THE NURSE, LIFE CHANGES

He nodded his head in the affirmative and Patricia helped him with the rest of his meal. She could tell he was worn out and lowered the head of his bed.

"Let me turn you slightly to get you off your back and you can take a nap." Patricia got him into as comfortable position as one can be with bulky casts, rubbed his shoulders, smoothed his bed covers, and Reid was soon asleep.

When he woke up, she would take his temperature and it would be time for some more antibiotics and pain medication. His face was healing nicely and the swelling was going down. He still had some discoloration. Patricia looked down at him. *He was a handsome man. There was something vaguely familiar about him. Oh, I suppose it is being with him since his surgery. He is bound to look familiar.* She charted how much he had eaten and drank.

Tomorrow they would do some labs on him and start reducing the pain medication. Since he ate today, he could take his medication orally and have the IV removed; otherwise they would have to change the site since this one had been in for almost seventy-two hours.

From his bed, she could hear Reid mumbling. She leaned closer thinking he might be in pain.

"Don't know…stop…" He appeared agitated.

"Are you okay, Reid?" Patricia put her hand on his shoulder.

Beads of sweat were on his forehead. He didn't answer.

Harry joined Patricia by the bed, "Anything the matter?"

"He was moaning, and all I could hear was, 'don't know, stop'. He might be reliving the beating he received."

"If you hear anything else, names, anything, James and I need to know." Harry looked at Patricia, "We want to bring them to justice."

"Why does he need you two as body guards way out here in basically wilderness? Who is he? Why would someone want to injure him so severely that they almost killed him?"

"I'm not at liberty to talk with you about this. Just let me assure you that Reid is a good person and hasn't done anything illegal. I will do anything to make sure no one ever does a number on him like this again." With that, Harry walked out of the room. He turned back, and said, "I'm going to take a walk around the building. I'm within shouting distance if you need me, and James is in the kitchen."

Patricia sat down in the recliner and looked at the sleeping man. What an enigma. *So, Reid isn't a criminal, but then Dr. Deerwater said that already. Yet Reid must be important to someone who is paying big bucks for his care. Was he related to someone in politics or is he one of those people who testify and they gave him a new identity? That would explain using both Harry and James for security. Well, I guess if they want me to know, they will tell me. Otherwise, it's my job to see that this man heals properly.*

Someplace in the house, the phone rang twice. Then Patricia was startled when the phone in the room rang. Patricia picked it up. "Hello, Nurse O'Malley, speaking."

"Hello, Patricia, Dr. Deerwater here. How is our patient doing?"

"He is improving chief. He ate oatmeal this morning and kept it down, so I say no more liquid diet. We had planned on doing some lab work on him tomorrow, and taking out the IV. Is that acceptable to you?"

"Is he still running a temperature?"

"It runs between 100 and 101."

"I think taking out the IV at any time would be okay as long as he is taking nourishment, and that should free up that left arm. Keep him on oral antibiotics until I come out to see him. There is still infection somewhere to keep his temp up. I believe I sent some with his medicine package. How is the laceration healing on the arm?"

"That, Chief is healing up nicely. His face looks wonderful too; you and Paul did a fantastic piece of surgery. Although he still has some black and blue areas from the beating, the swelling is coming down and the incisions look fine. Reid is breathing normally so that nose repair was right on. He hasn't commented on his vision at all, but then he hasn't used his eyes to read. Do you know if he wore glasses before? How old is he?" Patricia paused.

The Chief was laughing. "Oh, Patricia. Why not ask him how old he is. I'm glad he is progressing so nicely. I do plan to fly there in two weeks. I think we can take off his casts at that time and start some physical therapy on his arm and leg. You do know that Joe is a licensed physical therapist? Oh, by the way, I'm forwarding your mail, but if it's okay with you and Paul, I will open your utility bills and pay them and your rent. Have Paul send me an email if that is okay with him. That way, there won't be a late penalty to pay if I sent those to you and you and them back. Keep in touch, I have to go. They are calling me for surgery." The phone went silent.

CHAPTER TWENTY-TWO

Remove The Casts

"Time for lunch and we're going to have it on the porch. You're going to enjoy it out there. It is so beautiful, I just love this place. We need to put on this hat so the sun doesn't do a job on that handsome face of yours." Patricia produced a tan canvas hat with a wide brim.

"That hat looks more like I'm going on a safari than just to the porch." Reid gave a chuckle.

"I haven't seen any zebras or elephants but Joe says there are mountain lions around here. Hang on; let's see if the wheel chair can do wheelies." Patricia gave the wheelchair a push, but walked normally with it.

They bypassed the kitchen and went straight to the screened-in porch. There was a slight breeze and low humidity with the sun at high noon. With its rays filtered by the leaves on the trees, it was very peaceful. Over to the right were the vegetable and herb garden that Sierra used in her cooking. Straight ahead, nestled in a small grove of trees, was Sierra and Joe's cabin.

Making sure Reid's face was protected from the sun, Patricia turned to leave. "I'll go see if Sierra needs help with the lunch."

"Please stay a minute." Reid requested with his still hoarse voice."

Patricia sat down next to him. "What's up?"

"Do you know if my voice will ever get back to normal?"

"I can't answer that for sure. Sometimes when the nerves by the vocal cords get damaged, they do get better over time. Other times, they don't and some people lose all of their voice, which luckily, you didn't. It will just take time before you will know for sure. Dr. Deerwater is flying in today and we can let him assess it. Plus, if all goes well, he plans on taking off your casts and we'll start your physical therapy, get you back to your old self again. Isn't that good news?" Patricia's voice was full of anticipation.

Reid didn't respond, just sat there.

Patricia wondered what was going through his mind. She thought that getting the heavy, clumsy casts off would be welcoming news for him.

"Hey O'Patient of mine, where's the smile for the good news?" She gave him a hug around his shoulders.

He caught her hand, "I don't know that old self anymore." He dropped his hand back to his lap.

Kneeling down next to his chair, she asked softly, "Do you want to talk about it? Do you remember your past before the beating you received?"

He waved his hand through the air with a hopeless gesture.

The sound of a helicopter overhead shattered the moment. Dr. Deerwater had arrived and Patricia was very glad the Chief was here. There was more than the broken body that needed healing.

***

Paul and Patricia stood next to the table in the exam room as Dr. Deerwater began to cutting away the arm cast. The sound of the saw was always unnerving to patients. The musty smell wasn't expected by them either as the old cast was removed.

"One cast off, one to go." Dr. Deerwater said cheerfully. "I bet that feels good to get off." He threw the two pieces in the waste container, and then felt along the arm and gently moved it up and down checking to make sure the healing was complete. "I can see we need to develop those muscles again, but this is normal considering they haven't been used with the cast on. So far the arm looks good."

Once again, the saw was put into action and the cast taken off the leg, ankle and heel area.

"Hum, it looks like we have a bit of a sore here on the back of your leg and heel. No problem, we can make that all better too." He moved the leg around. "The hard part is the rehabilitation of the muscles. You will work up a big sweat." Dr. Deerwater smiled at Reid. "You have come through extensive surgery and recovered nicely. Now with the physical therapy, you will decide how quickly you regain your strength."

"Sierra, come here please."

Sierra in her manner, quietly entered the room, dressed as usual in a long skirt with a colorful top.

"Yes, Gordon."

"Sierra, do you have any sarsaparilla bushes around?"

"Yes."

"Will you make up a paste for this leg, especially the heel, and also brew some chaparral tea for Reid to drink?" He turned to Reid, "It tastes horrible, so chew on a mint leaf afterwards, but it will do the trick for healing inside and out."

Dr. Deerwater looked up at Sierra, "While you're at it, would you kindly make up some ointment for his arm and leg. Reid will be starting therapy and the muscles are going to be calling out for him to stop."

"Wouldn't it be easier to give me a pain pill, Dr. Deerwater?" A look of skepticism was on Reid's face. *Indian medicine?*

"Trust me, it will knock out that low grade temp you've been running, heal this sore and strengthen you. I can only use this out here, not in the hospital where everything must come from the pharmacy. This is the Great Spirit's pharmacy. One our people have used for ages. Let me assure you, when all is said and done, you will see the wisdom of my choice. Now, let's go to the workout room and I'll introduce you to the torture chamber as you will want to call it. Joe has worked with many patients here to rehabilitate the body. We will do our part to make you whole again, but you will have to do your share."

After the first exercise session, Paul helped the sweating Reid take a shower, his first since his beating. Then they massaged his sore body and applied the salve that Sierra had made. After drinking the cup of medicinal tea, Reid had an expression on his face that would compete with a young child being forced to take a terrible tasting medicine.

Jamming some mint leaves into his mouth, Reid looked at Sierra, "Has anyone ever died from drinking this?"

With her eyes smiling, "No, you may wish to, until it works its magic and heals you." Taking the empty cup, she left the room.

Patricia watched as Reid laid back and fell into an exhausted, troubled sleep. She would have been surprised if she could have seen the images that were floating around in his mind…his friend Cody, then his arm around Patricia, soft beautiful Patricia, then the beating under the smiling ugly fleshy face of…Reid began threshing about the bed, "I'll kill you Big Jake!" He screamed out as loud as his raspy voice would allow him to.

Jumping out of the chair, Patricia went to the side of the bed and put her hand on his shoulder. "Reid, wake up, Reid, it's me, Patricia. Its okay, everything is okay. Dr. Deerwater, come here." Patricia raised her voice.

Soon, the room filled up with all those in hearing range.

"Do you think he is reacting to the herbal medicine?" Patricia looked at Dr. Deerwater.

"No. he is fighting some other demons. We can help him with those too, but he will have to be willing to give them up," was his quiet reply.

Totally awake now, Reid looked bewildered at those around his bed. His clothes and the bedding were drenched with sweat. He looked over at Henry, who shook his head no.

Patricia offered him some cold water to drink, then getting a basin of water, sponged off his face. She could feel him relaxing.

Paul took a clean pair of pajamas from the drawer. "I think you will feel better with a shower about now. We need to change those sheets too, they are pretty damp."

While Reid was taking his shower, Patricia put clean sheets on the bed and tidied up the room.

As Paul and Reid entered the room, Patricia could see Reid was feeling better. "Well, now that things have quieted down, I think we should partake of the wonderful meal Sierra has made. Tonight Red, we will let you ride down in the wheel chair. Tomorrow, you will use a crutch and walk everywhere."

THE CABIN, THE NURSE, LIFE CHANGES

During the meal, Dr. Deerwater announced, "Paul, I need you back by my side in surgery. Our man here is doing fine and there aren't any unforeseen medical problems that need your attention. I do hope you enjoyed your vacation." He smiled over at Paul.

"Patricia, you'll stay here. Reid will still need some monitoring and you and Joe will see to his physical therapy routine. Harry and James will be all over the place, and if you need anything Reid, you just call out. Patricia will still be in her room, but no longer will be by your side unless you need her for something."

"Reid, you will continue on with the herbal drink and salve until your leg is totally healed. Your face is doing fine, the scars will fade more, stay out of the direct sun. The eye test yesterday showed no problems. You have been very blessed young man. Since Paul and I will leave in the morning, do you have any questions?"

"How long will I remain here?"

"About six weeks should take care of your physical therapy. Then, you shall be free to go wherever you wish." Dr. Deerwater smiled at him. "Well, if you will excuse me, I need to retire early. It has been a long week, and the helicopter will be here at five a.m. Good night all, and may you have a restful night."

"Reid, if you are finished eating, Harry and I will take you out to the front porch. There is a nice view out there and give Paul and Patricia a few minutes to chat." James began to push the wheel chair.

The three men went back through the house and out the front entry unto the porch. It was very serene there as the day was slowing coming to a close, with a spectacular sunset.

When they were all seated, James spoke quietly, "Man, Reid, do you know that you spoke Big Jake's name out loud when you were dreaming this afternoon? I wonder if Patricia heard any of it or did it mean anything to her?"

"I did? I don't remember any of it. It was all a terrifying haze. Is he dead?"

"No, and a couple of his bullies got away too and that's why we are here. Until you are on your feet and can take care of yourself and have total recall, you will have to look at our mugs. Speaking of mugs, yours looks really good, yeah, I'd say better than before the surgery."

The men laughed, they had worked together for a long time.

"Man, we didn't think you were going to make. You really had us scared there for a while." Harry added. "We also have all the papers you need for a new identity, bank account, social security, family history, work history, the works. You just have to say where you want to relocate and we'll get a driver's license for you."

"What if Patricia puts two and two together, or I slip with another dream?" Reid asked.

"Guess we will cover that bridge when we get to it." Harry responded.

The sound of footsteps caused the men to stop that discussion.

Paul and Patricia entered the porch.

"I just wanted to say good-night and thanks for letting me being here to assist in your recovery. As the Chief said, we leave early in the morning and I don't want to disturb you all. Paul reached out to shake their hands.

"Oh, I think the sound of the helicopter will have us awake anyway, and I want to see if they leave any gorgeous movie stars here to recover." James made wiggly movements with his eyebrows.

Patricia gave him a gentle poke on the shoulder, "You

men! All of you just think of a woman as a pretty face and body."

"Not me." Reid spoke up. "I appreciate the qualities of someone like you who has goodness and beauty inside and out." He gave her a long steady look.

CHAPTER TWENTY-THREE

The Walk

Every morning at sunrise, Patricia found herself waking and going to the porch and praying as Joe prayed to his Spirit from his cabin doorway. Then she went back to her room to dress and start the new day.

This was turning into a regular vacation since Reid didn't require skilled nursing. She tried to help him remember when he had a nightmare, but those were lessening, as he grew stronger.

She was pleased to see Reid appreciate the surrounding and saw him taking a book from the shelf to read. He also spent a lot of time with Harry and James.

Patricia strolled down the hallway to the kitchen where the freshly ground coffee beans made the air smell so wonderful. She inhaled the smell of it as the coffee pot perked away.

"Good morning. Ah, the smell of coffee makes me happy." Patricia smiled as Sierra poured coffee into a mug and handed it to her.

Pouring in some cream Patricia took a sip, "Um, thank you, Sierra."

"You're welcome." Sierra reached for an apron and tied it around her slim waist. "I was planning on cantaloupe, scrambled eggs and toast. How does that sound to everyone?"

"Perfect. May I help with something, like cut up the cantaloupe?" Patricia offered.

"Thank you that would be nice." Sierra slid the cantaloupe and cutting board closer to Patricia.

As the two women worked side by side, the men one by one came into the room, took a mug off the cup rack, and helped themselves to coffee.

James took a sip of coffee, leaned back against his chair and sighed, "If I could find a woman who could make coffee as good as you do, Sierra, I think I'd get married."

Everyone laughed.

"You are in luck, James. Patricia made the coffee today and she isn't married." She winked at Patricia merriment dancing in her eyes.

Harry raised up his hand, "Nah, not James, I'm the one she should marry. I'm good looking, charming…"

The hoarse voice of Reid interrupted, "If it's good looking, I win hands down with my new face." He said to a blushing Patricia.

Looking at Reid, Patricia didn't know what to make of his expression …warmth in his smile, but it was the sincerity in his eyes, and it reminded her of Hal. She knew the other men were kidding and she should laugh, but Reid wasn't kidding, and she was touched. She turned around to the counter, tears in her eyes.

Joe came to her rescue. "Men, I have been one lucky man. Sierra has shared my teepee, my lodge for many years.

THE WALK

Coffee wasn't the main reason we joined in marriage."

"Enough talk, time to eat or I feed it to the birds." Sierra placed the platters of food on the table and sat down with them.

Patricia took the empty chair by Reid.

"How are you feeling today, Reid? Is your strength coming back enough that we can forgo that marvelous chaparral tea?" Patricia looked at Reid.

"I will be your slave for life, Patricia if we can discontinue that foul tasting tea. No offense, Sierra, but it's horrible, even chewing mint leaves afterwards. Reid looked at one and then the other lady.

"What do you think, Joe? His temp has been normal for a while, the sores have healed; are the muscles coming back with the therapy?" Patricia took another bite of her food.

"Yes, the muscles are responding nicely. We are actually working on the whole body now." He looked over at Reid, "You must have worked out and had your body in great shape before the beating. I suggest, Reid; you have some alfalfa tea now to cleanse the rest of the body. It tastes good; I drink it myself at times with a little honey in it. I also think it will be okay to be more active than we have been by walking around the lodge and using the exercise equipment. We can all take a small hike after breakfast and see how the different terrain tests your limbs."

"I'll stay behind and keep an eye on the ole homestead," Harry smiled, "Someone has to watch over that jar of cookies Sierra made yesterday."

"And that jar better be full when we return or you will have to drink some Chaparral tea without the mint leaves to chew afterwards." Sierra threatened Harry in a non-threatening tone.

"What if we all meet back here in about fifteen

minutes? Put on some study shoes and wear a hat." Joe told them.

Fifteen minutes later, they all assembled back in the kitchen. Each one grabbed a walking stick from the old milk can on the porch and they were off.

Joe and Sierra lead the way, Reid, and Patricia next and James brought up the rear.

Patricia had an odd feeling as she observed a shoulder holster under James's vest and a walkie talkie in the side pocket.

As they walked, she thought back to the time when her leg was in a cast and she was at Hal's sister's home. There were enough guns around there too. She had been frightened, but Hal protected her when the crooks broke in. She missed him. They had some wonderful times when she wasn't studying or doing clinical. They loved to dance and had even taken dance classes.

Reid stumbled and Patricia grabbed his arm.

"Thanks, I didn't watch where I was walking, and tripped over that small stone. Do you think I should take it as a souvenir of my first hike?"

Joe looked at Patricia, and they both nodded no.

"I think mother earth wants to keep her rock and I think it is time we headed back to the lodge. Did you want to rest first, I know that small hill must have seemed very large to you and used some leg muscles that will complain later." Joe smiled at Reid.

"Yes, maybe we should turn back, it has felt good though to stretch out and feel the sun on my back." Reid wasn't stupid; he didn't want to overdo it.

"How about holding hands or linking arm? It might give you a little more balance on the rough ground." Patricia asked Reid.

"Thanks."

They went back the way they came, Joe and Sierra in front, Reid and Patricia next and James bringing up the rear.

Every so often, with the rough terrain, Reid would bump against Patricia and she would steady him. She actually liked the contact. Again, she was reminded of Hal. *Where was he? If he was alive and cared for her, loved her like he said he did, why didn't he get in touch? Or, maybe he wasn't alive.* Her heart sank. *She wanted to be loyal to Hal, and yet she was having feeling toward Reid. Hal had been missing for one long year.*

"You're very quiet. Are you okay? You seem miles away from here?" Reid squeezed her arm. "Missing the town life?"

"No, not the town life, a special person, you remind me of him."

"He must be one swell guy to have you thinking about him. Look, there's Harry lounging in the rocking chair. I sure hope he didn't forget to stir the soup or we will be eating peanut butter and jelly sandwiches." Reid joked.

Patricia stopped walking. *Hal liked peanut butter and jelly sandwiches.*

CHAPTER TWENTY-FOUR

Entertainment

The beautiful rose hues of the sunset were being ignored as James and Harry strolled down the horseshoe shaped driveway.

"When we started back from the walk today, I turned around and I'm positive I saw some mirror flashing. It didn't seem to be any Morse code message. Someone might be watching the lodge. I haven't seen any unusual signs when I've walked around and Joe hasn't volunteered any information either as to seeing others about, or anything we need to know. James commented.

"Yeah, I saw it too. I stepped back and used the binoculars but didn't see anybody out there and it was only a few flashes. Maybe we need to talk with Joe." Harry replied. "I saw him head for the garage not long ago, he might still be there."

As they entered the garage, both men swept the room with their eyes and only saw Joe there.

"Hey, Joe, you didn't happen to see anything out of the ordinary when we took our walk today did you?" James leaned against the wood support pole.

Joe grinned at the two men. "I saw the flashing and I know who held the mirrors."

James and Harry looked at each other and back at Joe.

"I don't suppose you would care to elaborate on that a little bit?" James asked as he pushed himself away from the pole. He didn't take guarding Reid lightly.

"Gordon has many relatives around here, and they all keep a watch on the place. Some of his patients want total seclusion and being in the public eye, there is always a chance of the press finding out and harassing them or damaging the property. Since Gordon knew your friend would be watched over by you two, he thought having our people help out behind the scene was a good idea." Joe grinned. "The message by the way said, 'everything is okay'."

"We appreciate your help, but it sure would have been nice if you had mentioned it to us when we got the layout of the land." Harry smiled. "I could have put my feet up and read a book and ate those cookies Sierra bakes instead of guarding the place like it is Fort Knox."

"Yea, I thought I was getting paranoid because, I thought I saw shadows and movements at night, but then, when we switched shifts, I'd check outside and didn't find anything to confirm my suspicions. Then I thought perhaps it was the spirits of your ancestors roaming around and I figured they must be good ones if they liked this area." James waited for some teaching on the spirit theory.

"You are right. We do ask our ancestors in the spirit world to watch over us at night, just as you pray to your God. We have many spirits. Sometimes we help them with our physical bodies." Joe was serious.

"Are those men out there armed?"

"Not to worry, James. The ones in the hills are, this is part of the reservation and we can carry our rifles, and besides, there are wild animals out there. The ones closer to the grounds only carry knives, but they are trained in martial arts. Usually all they have to do is take away a photographer's camera and the uninvited are ready to leave." Joe's response put the men at ease.

"How does the press find their way here if people want to heal in privacy? I was under the impression that this was Dr. Deerwater's private residence." Harry questioned.

"You know the movie stars. They mention going on a vacation to the hairdresser, a family member, or call home from here, and someone blabs or lets it slip when questioned by the press. There are no gates coming onto the reservation, so anyone could look around. We aren't that far from Cortez. This is beautiful country and there are a lot of places to see and things to do in this area. The weather is perfect and has an average temperature of 70 degrees. Drive a few miles north and you are in the mountains, go to the south and you are in desert area." Joe put the tools back on the pegboard that he had used fixing the window screen he had been working on as they talked.

"Well, I guess that makes our work a little easier knowing we have assistants standing by." Harry closed the garage door behind the men.

"I don't think we need to mention this conversation to Reid, let him work on healing, inside and out. Okay?" James looked at each man in the twilight.

Both men nodded in the affirmative.

Approaching the lodge, they could hear someone playing the piano. They looked at each other; no one had played it since they arrived except for Dr. Deerwater when he had made his short visit here.

Quietly entering the great room, they saw Reid and Patricia sitting together on the piano bench doing their rendition of chopsticks and laughing.

"Does this mean we are in for a concert tonight?" James asked startling the two.

"Of course. We were just warming up." Patricia giggled and bumped Reid gently with her shoulder.

"Can you wait and I'll see if Serena has any popcorn? James asked.

"I don't know. If this is a concert, you have to forego the popcorn. Popcorn is for movies." Reid joined in with laughter. His voice wasn't so hoarse; it was easier to understand him.

"But I want some popcorn." James stood looking at them with his hands on his hips.

They all laughed at his pouting.

"Go for it then while we plan our program for the evening." Reid pointed his arm toward the hallway that leads to the kitchen. "Joe, you and Sierra are invited to listen. We won't be offended if you wear ear plugs, since neither of us has played in years."

Reid and Patricia burst out in laughter. Reid put his arm around Patricia, "But we will give it our best with this short notice."

Patricia leaned her head on his shoulder, looked up and touched her hand to her brow, and with a dramatic Betty Davis voice said, "Yes, the great pianists, Mr. Reid and Ms. Patricia, will perform to a select audience tonight." Reid and Patricia looked at each other and broke out in peals of laughter like it was a private joke.

While Sierra was getting the popcorn and beverages ready, Reid and Patricia were going through some of the sheet music that they found in the piano bench. Some actually had notes from singers who had been there.

"So, how should we do this? Each one play a section, or just do it together? I haven't played in about two years, but I think I remember the notes." Again this struck them funny and they started laugh.

"Let's do it together and if you feel like you want to improvise at any point, go for it. I've played some but not regular since my friend Hal disappeared and I've worked with Dr. Deerwater. He is one busy surgeon. I'm pretty rusty myself. If we play together, maybe our nonpaying audience won't know which one of us hit a wrong note."

Patricia's reference to Hal took him off guard for a minute before he replied, "They will think we are pros, I think the guys have a tin ear." He hoped she didn't notice his hesitation in replying.

The rest of their group followed the smell of the popcorn and all settled on the comfortable couches and chairs, ready for the music.

"Don't we get any popcorn?" Reid looked at them.

"Nope, not till after the concert, and then if we aren't satisfied, you go to bed without any." James tossed a piece of popcorn into the air and caught it in his mouth. "We are a sophisticated audience I'll have you know."

Reid and Patricia stood up by the piano.

"Welcome to the special rendition of *Oklahoma*. Please feel free to join in loudly if you know the lyrics. May I introduce you to Mr. Reid on the lower keyboard, and myself, Ms. Patricia playing most of the melody."

They both bowed as their audience clapped, then took their positions at the keyboard.

The audience were all swaying back and forth as they sang. They were all enjoying themselves and the room resounding with the harmony of the voices.

The last few lines of the song *Oklahoma* brought the close of the concert. A delightful evening was held by all. As the rest left humming the tunes, Reid and Patricia went and sat by the fire that still had a few glowing embers burning.

"I guess our first concert was a success. I guess none of them have had any musical training or we would have been pelted with popcorn." Patricia laughed. "My friend Hal and I use to play together for fun. You have some of the same mannerisms that he did. It made it easy to accompany you."

"I was surprised that the notes and technique came back to me." Reid sighed.

"You had a lot of trauma to your head, and things will slowly come back to you. Maybe you should come out and play more often and see if that helps." Patricia patted his hand, "For now, I think we both need to turn in for the night. Joe has more strengthening exercises for you to do tomorrow."

"I concur. Let me walk you to your room." Reid offered her his arm.

"Thank you kind Sir, your gallantry is so appreciated."

They stopped by her open door.

"May I give you a hug of gratitude for a wonderful evening and making me look good on the keyboard?"

"I would like that. It was a nice evening."

At that moment, James came to his doorway, cleared his throat, "Ah, am I supposed to chaperone here or what?"

Reid and Patricia jumped apart.

"I was just thanking her for putting up with my playing tonight. You may go back to sleep ole guard of Patricia's virtue."

The three laughed and each went to their own room.

CHAPTER TWENTY-FIVE

Bad Memories

Reid went right to sleep with the feeling of Patricia in his arms and the light scent of the fragrance she wore still lingering by him.

For the first time since this capture and torture, he was experiencing a pleasant dream. Floating in and out were remembrances from the first meeting in the cold cabin with her broken ankle, her hospital stay, and the time spent at his sister's home and a visit from a couple of Big Jake's hoodlums. The time they spent in those two years, building a bond that he hoped would lead to marriage, but he was the one that insisted she get her nursing degree and not feel obligated to him for her paid education, to his last message from Cody saying Patricia had graduated with honors.

He had taken just small assignments to allow more time to spend with Patricia. How he loved her. His family and friends adored her. He was one lucky man. She was so talented and enthusiastic about life. They rode bikes, went boating, took dance lessons and many times they took his nieces hiking with them. Some evening, they sat together, Patricia engrossed in her studies, and he reading. Often they played the piano, doing two part music and she was also quite proficient on the flute.

On the day Cody and Kayla were married and Patricia was the matron of honor, how he wished they had made it a double wedding. Patricia was beautiful in the pale blue gown as she slowly walked up the aisle of the church.

Then the day Captain Marlin called requesting his help in northern Colorado, at a small town not too far from where Cody's cabin was. There was some activity from the group that Big Jake controlled even though he was incarcerated. Not only was the gang into drug trafficking, but kidnapping for ransom. If they could capture this group, it would close the chapter on Big Jake and his scumbag henchmen.

For the past year, Reid slowly worked his way into the group, gaining their trust until the last trip. He went to the café where he usually left any information. As usual, he sat in a booth and had some coffee and pie. The waitress was also a plant of Captain Marlin. When she presented the bill, Reid would put any small note with information on the tray with the money. They would do the usual banter servers do with regular customers but if she mentioned any movie that was in town, he knew there would be a message for him in the men's bathroom under the sink top from the captain.

Although he had gone to the café by himself, he knew he was being observed. No one went alone anywhere. There wasn't any trust in the world of crime. Reid didn't know that Hank, one of the gang came in after he went to the bathroom. Just as Reid pulled out the note, Hank walked in.

"What's that in your hand?"

"Oh, just picking it up off the floor. It got stuck on my

shoe." Reid replied as he tossed it in the trash container. Then he proceeded to wash his hands.

"Yeah, then I guess you won't mind if I take a look at it." Hank sidled over by the wastepaper basket, keeping his eyes on Reid.

"No skin off my nose if you like to handle trash." Reid replied, looking at the mirror to see if he would or not.

"Hum. 'New shipment coming in. should be the last. Careful.' So, what's this mean?" Hank asked waving the note at Reid.

"How am I to know? For Pete's sake, I pick up some trash as you walk in and you ask me what the note means. I didn't even read it." Reid shrugged his shoulders and tossed the used paper towel into the basket.

"And I suppose it's a coincidence that we have a new shipment of cocaine coming in? I think we better go back and talk with the boys." Hank patted his jacket pocket, the one he carried his small gun in.

Reid led the way out of the room, with Hank close behind him.

The waitress called out to Reid, "next week's pie special is apple."

"Don't hold any for him, honey; we have a small trip to make." Hank said.

As they left the building, Reid hoped that she got the message and would let Captain Marlin know that something was wrong.

Reid didn't know how wrong it would be.

Back at the house, they questioned Reid.

"How come you find a message like that about a shipment of cocaine and we are getting one? Answer that." Ronco asked in slow clipped off words. "Who sent this to you?"

"Why do you keep saying I know about it? I'm not the only one to use that restroom, and it's not exactly where the local high class goes to eat. I was just washing my hands and I hate messy things. You know how I keep my room clean." Reid was trying to buy some time. "For all I know the note was about the last shipment of fresh fruit coming in and the price was going up. I suppose the manager dropped it." He shrugged his shoulders.

"Take a seat. We don't know you all that well. You really haven't done anything to earn our total trust. You don't visit the whores, you don't get drunk or snort up once in a while and you didn't volunteer to cut off the ear of that kid whose rich grandpa didn't want to ante up some bucks. Why?" Ronco's voice was very deep.

"Aren't you getting a little excited about a piece of paper?" Reid smiled.

His smile vanished when Ronco pushed him back into the kitchen chair.

"This isn't a game. I didn't trust you from the start and I want some answers."

"First question, I don't visit whores, cause I don't like used merchandise. I don't get drunk or high because mistakes are made when under the influence of those. We need to keep our wits about us in this business. I didn't cut off the ear of the kids because it wouldn't make any difference in the outcome. He was his grandpa's favorite and the old man was going to pay anyway. It takes time to cash in stocks to get that kind of money." Reid sure hope he sounded convincing. He knew if he said anything acknowledging the note, the waitress would either be beaten or killed for more information.

That hope vanished when Ronco said, "Tie him up."

Reid slowly stood up. "That's not necessary, Ronco. Are you getting paranoid? I'm in this racket just like you are to make some easy money."

Roughly, Ronco pushed him back into the chair and the men held him as Reid tried to get up.

"Tie him up I said, tight." Ronco growled at the men.

Hank retrieved some clothesline rope and wrapped it around Reid's wrists and then around his arms and chest.

The questioning started over again. Each unanswered question resulted with a fist to the face. It wasn't long and Reid's face was a bloody mess. When the men saw that wasn't getting them anywhere, they brought out a bat, and he was beaten with that from his head down his body. Unconscious, Reid's head fell back and once more the bat came down and hit his chin and throat.

"He's done for, Ronco. He ain't gonna say anything, anymore." A sweating blood splattered Hank said. "I think we need to drop him off someplace and get out of here."

"Yeah, cut him loose and roll him in that rug, it will be easier for you and the boys to carry him out. Drop him anywhere. No one could recognize him anymore. Then meet me back here and we'll pack up and head for the cabin." Ronco dropped down into a chair and lit a cigarette, and rubbed his knuckles. "Oh yeah, take that bloody bat with you."

***

As soon as Hank and Reid left the restaurant, Shelly, the waitress immediately contacted the Captain and sent out a call to her partner. Then she hung up her apron, slipped into black jeans and an old well-worn leather jacket. Minutes later her partner, Dean pulled up in front of the cafe. Shelly quickly slid into the front seat and they headed for the house where the criminals were staying. Reid had passed that information to the Captain earlier when the gang has accepted him in.

It was dark by the time they got to that rundown

neighborhood. Parking around the corner to avoid being seen, they checked their weapons and left the car. They crept up to the bushes by the house and hid in the shadows. Shelly sucked in her breath when they observed three men struggle as they carried a rolled up carpet and put it in the back of a black SUV.

"Stick together or separate?" She asked her partner, Dean.

"Stick together and follow that SUV. There's someone in that carpet and I'm afraid it might be Reid."

They watched as the SUV went straight ahead and ran back to their vehicle. They soon located the SUV, but stayed far enough behind not to be noticed. The vehicle pulled over to the entrance that leads to the city dump. Shelly and Dean drove by and when they could, shut off their lights and backed up until they were concealed by a grove of trees and waited and watched.

"Did you get the license plates number, Shelly." Dean asked.

"Ah huh. I'll call it in and the description of the SUV to the boys. They can be waiting for them at the end of the road. We'll need the ambulance too." She called and was notified that help was on the way.

It wasn't long and the SUV pulled back onto the road and turned back towards town. Shelly and Dean waited until they were out of sight and then drove into the dump and the bumpy road. They put on the search light and it didn't take long to locate the rolled up rug with Reid in it.

They quickly exited the vehicle and ran to the rug. They unrolled it to reveal the bloody body. Shelly turned away and threw up.

"My God, Dean, I think he is dead." Checking his pulse it was very weak and his breathing was so shallow, he was barely alive.

The haunting wail of the ambulance was coming closer and getting louder, all the while Shelly was crying, telling Reid, "Hang on, hang on, don't die! You can do it. Don't let them creeps win. We'll get those lowlifes."

The ambulance took him to the Emergency Department and they registered him as Mr. Jones. As soon as stabilizing care was given, two undercover CIA men and a government helicopter picked up Reid and he was flown to the hospital where Dr. Deerwater had his practice. The doctor had assisted others from the government that needed his expertise from injuries in the line of duty. If anyone could save his life and make it worth living, not as a monster, it was Dr. Deerwater.

***

"Stop! Stop!" Reid's frantic, slightly hoarse cry shattered the stillness of the night.

The first one to his bedside was Patricia, followed by James and Harry.

"It's okay, Reid, I'm here. It's okay." Patricia crooned softly as she as she slowly rubbed his shoulder and arm.

Reid opened his eyes and looked bewildered.

"It was another flashback I think." Harry said from the other side of the bed.

Reid wiped the sweat from his brow with his sleeve. "I can't take those nightmares, the beating all over again."

Joe walked up to Reid and pulling a chair closer to the bed, straddled it and put his hand over Reid's. In a soft voice, "Man, you need to get rid of the demons in your head. We want to bring back the good memories, not the bad."

"Joe, I'm afraid to go to sleep nights. I never know when the bad ones are going to creep in." Reid's face registered fear and depression. "I can't keep on like this. I just can't."

Joe continued in his low soft voice, "As we used some of the Indian medicine to heal your body, would you be willing to try some for you mind? You are almost ready to leave here. You can do your physical therapy anyplace now and continue with your regular exercise regimen."

"I'm willing to try anything. I need to be free and whole, body and soul. There have been enough changes in my life. When do we start?"

"Tomorrow." Joe reached for the cup of chamomile tea that Sierra had silently appeared with. "This will help you to fall into a nice sleep. Tomorrow we talk." Joe stood up, nodded to the rest and he and Sierra left the room.

"I'll stay here with Reid; you two go back and get some shuteye." Patricia pulled the rocking chair over to the bed.

James and Harry looked at each other and said in unison, "Good night you two. Guess we know who the boss is around here."

"Finish the tea, Reid. I'll be right here." Patricia smiled at him.

"I feel like a big baby." Reid said as he handed her the empty cup.

"Then maybe I should sing you a nice lullaby." Patricia laughed. "Turn over and let me give you a back rub."

Reid did as she said, and with the combination of the tea and her soothing touch he was soon fast asleep.

Retrieving a soft blanket from her room, Patricia settled into the rocking chair and soon joined him in a deep sleep.

As the morning sun slowly chased away the night, Reid awoke refreshed. He looked over and saw Patricia peacefully sleeping in the chair, wrapped in the blue blanket.

He felt guilty that she spent the night there. He longed to take her in his arms and kiss her awake. *Would that ever be possible?*

Reid quietly slipped out of bed, gathered up his clothes, and went to take a shower. He remembered the talk with Joe last night and was excited and apprehensive as to what he had planned for today. Whatever it was, Reid was ready to try it, even if it included drinking some of that terrible tasting tea or something like it. He shuddered. As it was now, living with the nightmares wasn't living.

CHAPTER TWENTY-SIX

The Healing Begins

Deeper in the hills, away from Dr. Deerwater's lodge, Reid, Joe, and the shaman, Running Eagle, stood by the sweat lodge that Joe had built for his own use. It was actually a small teepee.

Reid was use to observing people and summed up a person's character rather quickly. He looked at Running Eagle, the spiritual leader for those in this area for the Ute Indians and felt at ease with him. Running Eagle was an older man of medium build with a quiet strength about him. Reid looked into his eyes, the soul of the man, and knew he was with a man that had faith.

"Last night, Joe gave me some hair from your brush and the hat you wear. I placed them on the blanket and asked the Great Spirit what was needed for your healing in here." He pointed at Reid's head, "And here," he touched Reid's chest.

"Tomorrow, we will build a fire in this sweat lodge and pray to the Great Spirit."

Running Eagle reached into the pocket of his vest and produced a small leather pouch, the size of an orange with a strip of rawhide threaded around the top with long ends tied so it could go over Reid's head. He held up the small bag. "Inside your medicine pouch is your own healing power. The Great Spirit pointed these out to me last night as I prayed for you. Hair from your head, for wisdom, herbs to sooth and heal, corn seeds as a symbol of new life, and a feather as a promise that the Great Spirit is there to guide and protect you. As I tie this around your neck, keep it with you. It is part of your sacred being." Running Eagle placed the leather strip holding he pouch around Reid's neck.

"To be sacred and purify, you need to step out of the secular world. Go bathe and fast from eating tonight, only consuming alfalfa tea for cleansing. Use this time to pray to your God, meditate on your healing. Take this and hang it from the window facing east to catch the bad dreams." Running Eagle handed Reid a dream catcher about eight inches in diameter. It was wrapped in leather, and had feathers and different colored beads worked into it. "Also, place your bed to face the east so you can greet Father Day when the sun rises. Get out of bed and praise the Spirit. Then come here and we will rid the evil from your body in the sweat lodge." Running Eagle nodded to both men, turned and silently on moccasin covered feet, disappeared into the forest.

***

Reid woke up as the sun was just appearing over the top of the mountain. He felt refreshed; pleased not to have had any of the horrible memories interrupt his sleep. He wondered about the dream catcher and he patted the leather pouch resting on his chest. *Were the Indian powers already working?*

Giving a morning prayer to God, he reached over to the table and picked up his Bible. Opening it up, the pages fluttered to the book of Psalms. Chapter 51 verse 10 stood out in bold letters like that verse was to be highlighted. He read it aloud, "Create in me a clean heart, Oh God and renew a right spirit within me."

Wow! Is that a coincidence or what? This has to be the day my life changes for the good. Is this all for real? He patted the leather pouch on his chest. His healing pouch.

Reid kept to himself, doing what he needed to prepare for his mental healing.

Everyone left him alone knowing this was an important time for him.

At the appointed time, the three met at the sweat lodge. Together they placed the wood inside the stone circle. Woven blankets lay on the ground to sit on. All preparation was accompanied with prayer.

When the fire was hot enough, the men took off their shirts and bending down, entered the teepee.

Joe poured some water over the stones causing the steam to fill the small area. It was hot in there. Joe began to drum with a steady beat.

Running Eagle stood up and began to dance to the beat around the fire, chanting, "Great Spirit be with us. Send in brother wind and blow away the evil spirit that may lurk within us. Fill us with your might power. The Great Spirit is our Father, The Earth is our Mother. She nourishes us. What we put into the ground she returns to us. Be with us, bless this young man, heal his head, erase the bad memories and fill his heart with love."

Joe and Reid joined Running Eagle in dancing around the fire, sweat rolling off their bodies, the Indian men with their chants, Reid with his white man prayers. The power filled the teepee and began to cleanse and heal. Reid was the first one to sit down; he was overcome with emotions that he couldn't explain except he had felt the touch of God like never before.

The years of dealing with the dregs of society and the almost fatal beating was falling away like chunks of black coal. The weight of anger, fear and hurt faded away. He felt free for the first time since working for the CIA.

Then Joe sat down with the shaman being the last to return to the blanket.

Running Eagle then picked up the pipe created from stone from the sacred Pipestone quarry in Pipestone, MN, and blessing the special tobacco, filled the pipe and lit it. He then stood up, to receive the blessing he inhaled deeply on the pipe and blew the smoke in six different directions, sat down and passed the pipe to Joe, who did the same and he passed it to Reid.

This was a new experience to Reid, but it seemed right, and he too followed in the ritual.

Running Eagle stood, stretched out his arms and prayed the Ute Prayer.

Ute Prayer

Earth teach me stillness
as the grasses are stilled with light.
Earth teach me suffering
as old stones suffer with memory
Earth teach me humility
as blossoms are humble with beginning.
Earth teach me caring
As the mother who secures her young
Earth teach me courage
as the tree which stands alone.
Earth teach me limitation

THE HEALING BEGINS

    as the ant which crawls on the ground.
    Earth teach me freedom
    as the eagle which soars in the sky.
    Earth teach me resignation
    as the leaves which die in the fall.
    Earth teach me regeneration
    as the seed which rises in the spring.
    Earth teach me to forget myself
    as melted snow forgets its life.
    Earth teach me to remember kindness
    as dry fields weep with rain.

Tears flowed down Reid's face, blending in with the sweat. He felt complete, whole, and not afraid.

Bending over, Running Eagle placed one hand on Reid's head, and raised his other toward the sky, "Great Spirit, we thank you and ask you to guide our brother as he leaves these hallowed walls."

At that moment, Reid felt a jolt go through him from the top of his head down to his toes. He would never ever be able to deny the power of God.

Running Eagle quietly left the teepee, followed by Joe.

Reid sat there until the teepee grew cool, giving praise to God, and the Great Spirit. He wanted to makes sure the Great One was thanked no matter by what name He is called.

CHAPTER TWENTY-SEVEN

The Truth Revealed

Patricia watched from the porch as Reid came down the path. He had a different attitude about him. He seemed relaxed, a serene look about him. She also noticed that he wasn't walking with a limp, but striding along.

She pushed opened the screen door and walked to meet him. She stopped and Reid took the next few steps, picked her up and swung her around in a circle. He put her down, giving her a huge smile.

"I have never felt so free in all my life! I just know I am a changed man forever."

"I'm so happy for you Reid. Do you know you aren't favoring your leg?"

"Patricia, I don't know how to explain it, but when the shaman was praying, I felt an energy go through me from my head to my toes. I truly believe I'm totally healed, inside and out!"

Reid's face was wreathed in the biggest smile Patricia

had ever seen.

She hugged him. "This is what you desired and you have been blessed."

They entered the porch hand and hand.

"We received some mail from Dr. Deerwater today. There is an envelope addressed to you. I didn't know that anyone knew you were here." She gave him a questioning look.

"Neither did I." He replied.

They went into the living room and she handed over the envelope. He took it to his room to read in private. He wasn't sure what to think. Only Captain Marlin knew he was here. He slid the blade of his pocket knife under the seal and pulled out the letter. A picture fluttered to the floor. Bending over he picked it up surprised to see Cody, Kayla, the twins and their new son Andrew. They were all smiling. Gosh, he missed his friends. He might never see them again in person.

Sitting down in the rocking chair, he began to read the letter.

"Dear Hal,

Captain Marlin met me and said you had been beaten pretty bad by the perps, but were expected to live now, for which we are very grateful.

He also said I could contact you through the doctor that repaired your face. Guess you're as handsome as me now. Ha ha.

I don't know where you are to relocate, but perhaps when some time lapses, we can get together. If they did a super job on your face, you might not even be noticed around here and could stay close to home. Is that an option?

Your sister got a personal visit from the captain and a notice was put in the obituary column about your death. She knows the truth but did a good job of crying at the memorial

THE CABIN, THE NURSE, LIFE CHANGES

service. We had the place covered, but didn't see any of Big Jake's goons.

Speaking of big Jake, here is some good news. Our ole nemesis Big Jake is residing in the lower bowels of hell. One of the inmates didn't like the way Big Jake was pushing him around and held him down with his head in the toilet until there were no more bubbles coming up. Good riddance to a slim ball.

The girls are taking piano lessons and me, well since I quit the service; I'm doing what I always wanted to do, work with wood. Even made a few bucks already.

Kayla works as a substitute teacher so she can pick and choose when she wants to work and keeps her credential up to date. She doesn't want to work full time until Andrew goes to school even though I'm here for the kids.

I miss you buddy, you know you are like a brother to me. You can write me c/o Dr. Deerwater.

Love,

Cody and family."

Reid sat there with tears in his eyes blurring the faces in the picture. Had it been worth it to give his life to the CIA and end up like this? Would he ever be free to see his family again? He got up, put the letter and photo on the dresser and looked into the mirror. Did he resemble his old self? He peered closely. He couldn't see anything familiar about him. He dropped his head down.

Glancing into his room, Patricia saw Reid standing by the dresser with his head lowered. What had happened to the excited man of fifteen minutes ago? Did he receive some bad news?

He didn't hear her walk up to him, but felt her hand on his arm. He turned around.

"You okay, Reid?"

"Yeah, I am. It was good news."

Patricia looked over at the letter and saw the picture. She picked it up and looked at him. "How do you know Cody and his family?"

"Remember the beaten, broken man you helped repair in surgery? That was Hal. Dr. Deerwater turned Hal into Reid."

Patricia stood very still for a moment absorbing what he had just said. "Hal? My Hal? Oh my God! She sank to her knees and began to sob, "You're alive. You're alive!"

Reid knelt down and put his arms around her.

"Why didn't you tell me? I worried about you for that long year, not knowing if you were dead or alive."

"Patricia honey, you know how the CIA works. Do you know how hard it has been to be around you and not reveal this to you? I love you so much, I have for four years."

James and Harry stood at the door and soon were joined by Joe and Sierra. They all just watched, listened and didn't say a thing.

Patricia raised her hand and traced the outline of his face and lips. "I should have known. You did so many things like Hal. I was so dawn to you."

Reid took her hand and helped her to her feet, then noticed their audience at the door.

"So, it looks like the secrets out. What are you two going to do?" James asked for them all.

"See if my lips work." Reid said as he lowered his head and kissed Patricia, who in turn kissed him back.

Whistles went through the air and they all clapped their hands.

Everyone could tell there was love in the air and there were going to be some more life changes.

CHAPTER TWENTY-EIGHT

Dr. Deerwater

The soft, soothing music of the flute was playing as the team stood around the operating table. As he always did before surgery, Dr. Deerwater bowed his head and offered a prayer for the patient and the medical team.

"Adjust the light on your right, Karen," Dr. Deerwater requested.

"How's that Chief?" She looked over at him.

"Fine, just fine. Is everyone ready?" He looked at his special operating team assembled around the table and nearby. Beads of sweat covered Dr. Deerwater's forehead.

"Chief, are you feeling okay?" Karen asked as she patted away the sweat with a cotton pad, deposited it in the basket, and reached for clean gloves.

"I. I." He dropped the scalpel and grabbing his chest, fell against the table holding
the surgical instruments causing them to scatter, and slowly crumbled to the floor.

Paul Armstrong, the assisting doctor knelt down and shook Dr. Deerwater by the shoulders, "Chief, are you okay? Can you hear me?" He asked as he listened for breathing and checked for a pulse. "Call a Code Blue stat! He's in cardiac arrest!"

Grabbing a knife that had fallen on the floor from the tray, Paul cut open the doctor's operating scrubs to expose his chest. The crash cart was swiftly brought over from the corner and the surgical team immediately began CPR. Applying the pads, Paul looked around the group, "Clear?" "All clear" was the response and the shock was administered.

The second one got Dr. Deerwater's heart beating again.

Others responding to the Code Blue arrived. They lifted him onto a gurney, and moved him another room.

Dr. Armstrong looked around at his co-workers. "He's in good hands now. Let's say a prayer for him and those who feel we can do this surgery nod your head."

Everyone nodded in the affirmative. They were professionals and they had a patient counting on them to repair the damages done by the car accident.

Paul bowed his head, "Heavenly Father, one of your children needs your healing power right now. We ask that you be with him and the doctors attending. Thank you, Lord, in Jesus name we pray. Amen"

He looked over at the anesthesiologist, "How is our patient doing?"

"Fine, Paul."

"Okay everyone, let's scrub up again and continue with this patient. I don't want to keep our patient under too long. We should be ready in fifteen minutes."

All eyes turned to the large clock on the wall and left to scrub and suit up again.

Over the intercom in the OR came information on Dr. Deerwater's condition. "Team A. The CT scans shows Dr. Deerwater has suffered a coronary thrombosis, and we will be a doing triple bi-pass shortly. We will keep you posted. We don't anticipate any problems; he basically is a healthy man."

There was a collective sigh of relief that he was alive. They all made eye contact and then Paul picked up a scalpel from the tray.

***

The first thing Conrad saw as he left the fog from anesthesia was Patricia. *What was she doing here?* He raised his head, groaned, and laid back down. It was too much of an effort.

"Hello, Chief. Welcome back to the land of IV's and bedpans." Patricia took his hand in hers.

"What happened?" He looked up at her. "Why am I here, and when did you get here from the lodge?"

"Well, you decided to have some blockages in your coronary arteries and lost your place at the operating table as head surgeon, to be a patient instead. For the record, you breezed through it with no problems. And I'm here because they wanted your favorite nurse to boss you around. I couldn't miss that opportunity." She smiled at her friend.

With his right hand, he touched his chest and looked up at her, "Who did the surgery? I hope it was someone who does nice neat stitches."

They both laughed.

Peeking his head around the corner, Paul got the nod from Patricia and walked up to the bed. "Since you opted out of the surgery for our accident victim, I did a very good job. She will never know it wasn't you that did those nice small sutures on her face." Then, the smile disappeared, "Chief, from now on, no more long hours in the operating theater, and more relaxation time. Matter of fact, as soon as you get the okay, we are sending you home to your lodge for some needed R & R."

"And, I'm going with you." Patricia added, "Reid is there and Joe and Sierra are getting things ready for your arrival. You have no say in this matter." She smiled at him.

"Whatever you say." Conrad leaned his head back, closed his eyes and succumbed to the effects of his medication. Dr. Conrad (Chief) Deerwater was finding out what surgery and it's after effects felt like.

***

Taking advantage of being back in the city, Patricia called her brother to meet for coffee. They had a lot of catching up to do.

Ted could hear the phone ringing as he fumbled with the old lock on the door. *This darn lock, I'm ready to pay for a replacement myself!* After the third try, he heard it click, pushed the door open and swiftly walking, and grabbed the ringing phone. "Hello?"

"Hi Ted, it's me, Patricia. I was just about to hang up."

"I was struggling with that vintage lock. It's pretty, but worn out. It's great to hear your voice sis, it's been awhile. What's up at the lodge?"

"That's why I'm calling, I'm not at the lodge; I'm here at the hospital. Dr. Deerwater had open-heart surgery and they wanted me as his personal nurse. I'll be here until he is released and we go back to the lodge so he can recuperate surrounded by his people and in such a lovely, relaxing setting."

"What a rough job you have. I would describe it more as a vacation you get paid for." Ted chuckled. "Unlike mine where I do everything from helping to deliver animal babies to cleaning up manure from them, and recording what it looked like. Yep, I guess I should have gone into nursing."

"Yeah, well we have been known to do a few enemas in our field too you know." Patricia laughed. "Say, can we get together for some coffee here at the hospital? I should be here for a couple more days before we fly out to the lodge."

"Sure, I can get someone to cover for me. How about this afternoon around three, will that work for you?"

"That will work out fine. Dr. Deerwater should be napping and we can meet in his room. Third floor, room 310. Would you mind picking up some wonderful coffee with vanilla creamer in it? You know how blah the hospital coffee is." Patricia groaned.

"No problem, Sis. See you in a few hours. I've miss you."

"Oh, Ted."

"Yeah?"

"Wash your hands before you come…I don't want any animal doo doo on my coffee cup." Patricia laughed.

"Will do, I'll change clothes too. Bye Sis."

Patricia could hear him laughing as Ted hung up.

CHAPTER TWENTY-NINE

Visit With Ted

Patricia heard the elevator door open. The darn bell always sounded when the elevator stopped at a floor. She peered around the door into the corridor. There he was her big brother with cups of coffee in a holder and a bag that she bet held her favorite blueberry-cream muffin. She smiled as the nurses at the desk took notice of her handsome brother. She sighed. It wasn't anything new; Ted was always getting admiring glances from the female population.

"It's wonderful to see you, Bro," Patricia wrapped her arms around him with an embracing hug.

Ted was trying to balance the coffee and sack of muffins and give his sister a returning hug all at the same time. "I should have brought bananas, and then maybe I could have juggled all of this and you too. The monkeys at the zoo do a great job of grabbing things and they eat a lot of bananas." He gave her a gentle hug, careful not to spill the hot coffee on her.

Patricia backed away just far enough to retrieve the coffee holder from him. "I have missed you so much, Ted, almost as much as the coffee." Her eyes were full of laughter. She held the coffee up by her nose, "Um, and it smells so good. I think getting away from the zoo for a few hours is good for you, you know, to see how the rest of the world looks." She remarked with a soft tone chuckle, "And not from behind an animal."

"Gee, I'm sure glad you missed me." He took the coffee tray from her and placed that and the sack of muffins on the table; picked her up in a huge bear hug, swing her around and gently let her down. Taking both of her hands, he stepped back looking at her, "You're looking absolutely fab sis. Must be all the country living."

A blush covered Patricia's face.

"Yes, I've really taken a liking to the country living, and to the patient I've been taking care of there. That's what I wanted to talk to you about. Let's sit down." She pointed to the round wooded table with matching chairs in the corner of Dr. Deerwater's private room. She closed the door to the hallway for privacy.

The sun shone through the slanted blinds giving the light green walls a relaxing hue. The room was decorated like a living room except for the medical equipment that could be put behind a folded cupboard when not needed. The bedding had modern designs in it that complemented the green colored walls. There were a couple of original paintings hanging whose purchase must have made some hungry artists very happy. Private rooms were nice.

They sat down and removed the lids from the coffee cups releasing a puff of steam.

Patricia leaned over her cup and she sniffed the aroma. "Um, this smells heavenly."

VISIT WITH TED

Ted wrapped his hands around his cup and leaned forward. "I agree. Now spill, big brother is listening, what's been going on?"

"I've fallen in love with a special man and he has proposed to me." She placed her left hand on the table with the blue opal ring nestled in a delicate gold setting.

He looked at her with a quizzical expression, "Isn't that the ring Hal gave you four years ago? Doesn't his guy have enough money to buy you a ring?"

She nodded.

"I thought Hal was dead. I saw the obituary in the paper and gave my condolences to Cody and Hal's family. Why would you be wearing his ring if you're engaged to another man? Who is he? Where did you meet him? It hasn't been that long since Hal's death."

Concern showed on his face.

Patricia put her fingers up to her lips. "Shush." She looked around and leaned forward. "Remember the reason I went to the lodge?"

"Yeah, a patient of Dr. Deerwater was badly beaten and needed special care to recover and you went because you were single and could be away from home for while without it being a hardship on a family."

Patricia's face was very serious and she spoke so softly Ted strained to hear her.

"What I'm going to say you must never tell anyone. That barely alive man was Hal. He is now Reid, alive and well. As far as the world knows, Hal is dead. As Reid, if his true identity was ever known, his life would be in jeopardy again. The main criminals he caught are dead, but you never know in a world of crime what could surface. I couldn't bear to lose him again."

Thoughtfully, Ted leaned back into his chair, silent for

a moment. *This was quite a bit to digest. Hal was now Reid and his little sister was going to marry him.* Looking intently at her, "Pat, are you going to be in danger all the time? Look at what you have gone through already."

Shaking her head, "No, I won't be in trouble; it would be such a remote chance that anyone from his old life would recognize him. I didn't by looking at him. It was the little things, the feelings that I had, not his face. I was drawn to him before I knew who he was and felt guilty not knowing where Hal was. As I said before, he is a different person now, a new face, identity, the whole thing. It is a precaution so we won't have to live looking behind us constantly, living in fear. Now, you didn't say anything about me getting married."

"You know I'm happy for you. I know how crazy in love you two were, and there is no way I would ever stand in your way. When did you discover Hal and Reid were one and the same?"

"It was weird in away. I kept having these warm thoughts about him that I've never had about a patient before. I felt as if I knew him, yet felt guilty because I didn't know at the time if Hal was dead or alive. I thought what a coincidence that Reid and Hal were alike in so many ways." She paused a moment lost in memory.

Ted waited quietly.

Then Patricia continued with a smile. "You would have loved the night the two of us put on a concert for the rest of them at the lodge from the show, OKLAHOMA. I thought how natural it was for us to be playing together, just like Hal and I did, but it was Reid. It was a lovely night and at the end, he gave me a hug. I was in his arms, it felt so right and I didn't want the evening to end."

"Was that when you realized Hal and Reid were one and the same?" Ted took a sip of his coffee.

"No, I walked in one day and found pictures of Cody and his family and a letter on Reid's dresser. I was hurt and angry, but then Reid explained with the injuries and the nightmares that he had from the beating, he didn't think he could be the man Hal was and wanted me to be free to find someone else."

"That's amazing! So, where do you go from here?"

"That depends on Dr. Deerwater's recovery. When I'm not needed, Reid and I will be married. We both would like to have the wedding at the lodge. It's such a beautiful place with lovely memories for us. We can have you, Cody's family, and Reid's sister and family there. I can't wait!" She softly clapped her hands together her smile lighting up her face.

"I hope it's soon. I got an offer from a zoo in Australia that I would love to take. I was going to write you about it." Ted's face was full of excitement. "There are so many studies they want and I have become quite knowledgeable in my field."

Mixed emotions came to Patricia. *Australia? That was so far away.*

CHAPTER THIRTY

Conrad Picks A Nurse

Conrad leaned back in the old wooden rocker on the porch and gave a sigh of relief to be home. Although the helicopter ride had been smooth, he was tired. He shook his head, he thought he was stronger than he was and it bothered him that he was weak and his chest still hurt, this was totally understandable. How many times had he explained that to his patients? He didn't anticipate any problems with the bi-passes; he just needed to let things heal. It was good to be home. Then he smiled, but maybe not with Patricia, Sierra, and Karen hovering around him every minute. This was possibly the first time he had been alone since the heart attack, with the exception of going to the bathroom. Well, they walked him there and stood outside to assist him back to his chair or bed.

He could hear their voices from the living room as they planned his agenda for the next week. At the rate they were going, he would be lucky if they let him eat and not be spoon fed. He rocked back and forth, the colorful Indian blanket on

CONRAD PICKS A NURSE

the back of the rocker flowing back and forth with him. He was one lucky man to have so many people care about him, and not just because of his position as a surgeon.

The red and blue hues of the sunset filled him with a sense of peace. He slowly rose and stood with his hands on the railing and took a deep breath. Reaching into his pocket, he removed a small leather pouch, taking a pinch of tobacco, sprinkled some to the north, east, south and west. Then he slowly raised his arms toward the sky and chanted his prayer of thanksgiving to the Spirit of the sky.

Back in the living room, the women heard Conrad praying and ceased talking. They too bowed their head and each in their own belief gave thanks for the day.

When there had been a space of time and silence, Karen softly walked to the door. "Such a lovely sunset, I should take a picture of it. I can see why you love the peacefulness of your lodge. I hate to disturb your relaxation, Conrad, but it is time for your medication. I know it's your first night home and you would like to stay up longer, but I really think it's best for you to retire now. I don't want you to overdo it."

He turned his head slightly, "I think your correct, Karen. It has been a long day. Would you have Sierra brew me a cup of her special tea?" Carefully rising, he took her arm and they slowly walked down the hallway to his room.

Patricia and Sierra were smoothing down the covers on his bed. They were using the hospital bed to make it easier for him to get in and out. There on the nightstand was a mug of steaming tea, its mint aroma giving the room a peaceful feeling.

Conrad and Karen arm and arm stood in the doorway and laughed. "Do you read minds, Sierra? I had just asked Karen to have you get me a cup of tea, and like magic, here it is."

"Oh Conrad, how long have I known you? I think enough years to anticipate your wishes and what you like and don't like. Many times you have ordered this same tea for your patient's first night here." She smiled at her cousin and gently laid her hand on his arm. "Joe will be here if you need him tonight." She gave a pleasant nod to them both and quietly in her way walked out, her long blue skirt moving ever so slightly as she glided down the hall.

Karen looked over at Conrad, "Joe wasn't there when we picked straws to see who would stay the night with you. I got the short one. Are we to play cards here?" Her eyes questioned him. "I wonder why you asked me to be your nurse when you have Patricia here. I wasn't aware that your cousin and her husband also were trained as physical therapists and a dietician." She assisted him to his chair and then knelt down to remove his slippers.

"Karen, you're a skilled nurse familiar with heart surgery, I wanted you here in case some weird unexpected thing did happen and with all of you here, it could be dealt with expertise. I'm aware I came home much sooner than I should have." He put his hands on the upper part of her arms and held them firmly. "I also wanted you to see where I live, my life away from the city, to be with Conrad, not Dr. Deerwater or Chief as everyone so affectionately calls me. I wanted you to be here, with me. You as Karen, the woman. Tonight in your capacity as a nurse, take my vitals, give me my medication, then you can go rest, and Joe will be here, he also needs to be here. He is family. Do you understand?"

His brown eyes held her light blue ones in a search for an answer; he didn't need her to speak.

Her blond head nodded up and down slowly. She understood perfectly. *So she wasn't imagining things back at the hospital. He did like her, but never would have made any overtures to see her outside of the hospital because of hospital politics and the rumor mills.*

"Good. It pains me to see you unhappy." Conrad smiled at her.

Patricia slipped past them, "Guess you two don't need me anymore, if you do, I'll be in the great room with Reid at the piano. Any requests?" She gave them a wave of her hand, turned right at the door. *This was going to be an interesting three months.*

Reid rose from the chair as Patricia entered the room.

She walked over to him and slipped into his open arms.

Leaning down, he ever so gently kissed her on the lips. "I love you lady."

"Tell me again," She kissed him back.

"I love you lady, I can put it in writing too, like on a marriage license. What do you say about that? Will you marry me, soon?"

"Oh, yes, Reid. I love you so much."

Taking her hand, he led her to a chair. When she was seated, he knelt down, took her left hand in his and removed the beautiful blue opal from her finger.

"Reid, what are you doing with my ring?"

Reaching into his shirt pocket, he took out a gold engagement ring with one large diamond in the center and a smaller one on each side of it. Again he took her hand and slowly slid the ring on her finger. "The opal was a friendship ring. This one is for you to wear until I put the wedding band next to it and call you my wife."

Patricia slid off the chair into his arms and hugged him tight, tears coming down and wetting his shirt. She raised her head, "I have loved you for so long." She looked at the huge diamond ring on her left hand that sparkled in the light from the fireplace. Reaching for the blue opal, she put in on her right ring finger. "I have two rings you gave me with attached promises. With the opal, my nursing tuition was paid for, and now with this lovely engagement ring, our wedding, our future, with you my wonderful man will make my life complete." She put her arms around him and began to smother his face with kisses, murmuring, "I love you, I love you, I love you. Oh, Reid."

"Well future Mrs. Reid Jones, I think we need to set a date and make some plans."

"Ah huh, after a few more kisses, Mr. Jones."

"I'll be happy to oblige."

There were no musical requests played that night.

CHAPTER THIRTY-ONE

Wedding Plans

Reid and Patricia sat in the summer porch with their coffee. A pad of paper and pen were sitting on the table with some notes on it.

"I wrote down some ideas about the wedding to share with you. I think that we can have Cody, Kayla and children, your sister and family, and my brother. Of course, Joe, Sierra, and any patients that might be in residence would naturally be included. Doesn't it feel like Joe and Sierra are family?"

"That sounds fine with me, but what do you think of having Paul, and I would like Captain Martin, if he can make it here." Reid stirred the spoon around in his cup. The captain and I go back a long way, and Paul helped save my life."

Patricia took his hand and held it. "By all means, is there anyone else?"

"Not with my new identity, I couldn't risk it. I imagine you wanted a big fancy wedding with the many friends you've made. I'm sorry we can't."

"We will make new friends as Reid and Patricia, and I really don't want a big wedding. They get so complicated and stressful worrying about the show surrounding it instead of two people taking their vows." She smiled at him, "I would like to wear my mother's wedding dress. I've kept it all these years. It will probably need some alterations done. I know we haven't talked about what type of wedding, informal or not and I don't really care, except wearing her dress, I would feel like my mom was with me on our special day."

"You will make a beautiful bride in her dress. I want to wear a suit, but for everyone else, why not let them wear something that blends in with this location, you know, clothes like Sierra wears?"

"What a wonderful idea!" Patricia made a notation on her list. "Now, I assumed you would ask Cody to be your best man and I was going to ask Kayla since I was her maid of honor, yet I feel so close to Sierra since we have been here…" She tapped the pen against her chin.

"I heard you." Sierra stepped into the porch. "You give me great honor to consider me for this special occasion, but you need to have your friend Kayla by your side. She would have a heavy heart. Besides, I will be doing what I love to do, seeing that everyone is eating well and comfortable. If we have a patient here, I will also be taking care of their needs." She hugged Patricia and silently went back into the kitchen.

Patricia and Reid exchanged glances.

"I guess that problem is solved. Now, whom do we get to marry us? I know, we could have a judge, but I would prefer a minister, and also have Running Eagle do a blessing. Without his healing ceremony, I wouldn't be a man capable of being a husband, but a man living in fear. What do you think?" He was serious.

"Perfect. Why don't we ask Conrad if he knows of a

minister nearby? I don't know if they have clergy on the reservation or not. Do you have a preference of denomination?"

"No, in the line of work I was in, it was the belief in God that mattered, not the name on the church. Even now, see how much we have shared with Joe, Sierra and running Eagle. It must be someone who just thinks we are friend and colleague of Conrad's, just in case...You realize this is how we will live our lives, always wondering if we let something slip out, never sharing my past, matter of fact, we have to invent my past for strangers." He looked at her with sad eyes. "Do you really understand how much this will limit you?"

"I do, very much. But we have a new life ahead of us. Now, let's set a date. I want Ted to be here and if he accepts the offer to move to Australia, he needs to leave as soon as his passport and all the details are taken care of. Oh, you know, I need to go back to my apartment and pack, get my wedding dress, and let the landlord know I'm moving. Maybe I should keep it though for when I work at the hospital. What do you think?"

"We really don't need it. Conrad is letting us have the guest cottage, and you can stay with Kayla or my sister when you are in town, and you could always stay at Conrad's place when he is doing surgery. Let's run that by him when we ask about a minister." He gave her a real warm romantic smile, "And the date, how about three weeks from today? Do you think that is enough time to make all the arrangement? I wish it was tomorrow."

Patricia blushed and looked down at the calendar and marked the date with a big W. Looking sideways at him, "I feel the same way." She leaned over to meet his lips in a warm kiss. Then she straightened up. "Back to the wedding plans, how about we have the wedding in the late afternoon, just before the sunset. You know how beautiful it is at that time of the day." She reached for his hand and squeezed it. "Let's go talk with Conrad, and if the date and everything is okay with him. We can make the invitations on the computer and get them out yet today, or should we wait and see if we can locate a minister first?"

Standing up, Reid took her in his arms, "I think, my future Mrs. Jones that securing a minister is a rather important thing. Let's go find Conrad."

As they walked through the kitchen, Sierra said, "Then come see me and we will plan the menu, I have many ideas." She smiled at them and resumed slicing up vegetables.

Reid and Patricia turned around and Patricia gave Sierra a hug. "What would I do without you? You are such a dear person."

Hugging her back, Sierra whispered in her ear, "You are a special lady and I am pleased to mean so much to you."

"That goes for me too, Sierra. Your care and wonderful meals made me well." Reid put his arms around her with a warm hug.

Leaning back, Sierra's face radiated happiness, "You two better go talk with Conrad, three weeks will go by swiftly."

Taking Patricia's hand, Reid led the way out of the kitchen.

CHAPTER THIRTY-TWO

The Wedding Plans Continue

Reid and Patricia paused at the doorway to Conrad's room. Karen was perched on the bed next to Conrad looking at a photo album.

"Knock, knock, are you busy?" Patricia asked.

Quickly sliding off the bed, a blushing Karen nodded. Nurses don't sit on a patient's bed with them. "Conrad was showing me how the building of this lodge progressed. I didn't realize how the beams, and stones for the fireplace, so many things came from the land."

"We appreciate the architecture of the lodge too; that's why we are here." Patricia and Reid looked at each other.

"Conrad, what do you think of having the wedding three weeks from today? I know it is soon, but you should be feeling pretty good by that time, and we don't want to wait any longer."

Karen with smiles on her face first gave Patricia a big hug, then Reid. "Congratulations, I'm so happy for you!"

Conrad's laughter rang out. "I've been wondering when you two were going to finally set a date. What can I do to help?"

"We were wondering if you know of a minister that either serves the people on the reservation or is from town that could do the ceremony, but, we would also like to have Running Eagle do part of it or at least give us a blessing. Without his Spirit, I wouldn't be a free man able to ask this lovely lady to marry me and be the man she needs." Reid put his arm around Patricia and held her close.

"Yes, I know a priest, I'll give Father Jim a call and I'll have Joe get in touch with Running Eagle but don't be surprised if he would show up today. Somehow, that man has a sixth sense when he knows he is wanted or needed. Give me the exact date and time and I'll call Father Jim today. Now, who is going to give the bride away?" Conrad rubbed his hands together.

"I'm going to have my brother Ted. That's the reason we are choosing the date so soon. Ted is taking a position with a zoo in Australia. I need him to be here. He is the only family I have left."

"So, what do I get to do then? I was hoping to be the surrogate dad and walk you down the aisle. Oh, I know, I'll do what most dads' do... pick up the bill for the wedding. That is my gift to you both. Everything is on me." Conrad beamed and looked at everyone in the room.

"We can't let you do that; just having the ceremony here is enough." Patricia shook her head.

"It's not open for discussion; it is settled. Where do you want to purchase your wedding dress? Who is going with you?"

Patricia went to the bed, put her arms around Conrad and hugged him. "You are to wonderful, but I'm going to wear my mother's dress."

Reid took his turn to shake the man's hand. "All I can say is 'thank you', thank you from the bottom of my heart."

Conrad waved his hand, "This makes me happy to have a wedding in my home. Now, whom are you inviting? Will there be enough rooms here for everyone or do I need to fly them out at night? Talk with Sierra about the menu and if she needs help, she will call on the cousins. What type of flowers do you want? Where will the ceremony take place? Do we need a tent set up?" His voice was excited. He rubbed his hands together, he loved parties, especially here in his home. "Music, what type of music? Do we need musicians, canned music or drums?"

Karen placed her hand on Conrad's shoulder, "Hey, don't get so excited. Maybe I should take your blood pressure."

Conrad waved his hand, "I'm fine, perfectly fine. I'm just so happy for this couple. It's not every day I have a wedding at the lodge." He patted her hand. "Good happy is medicine for the heart."

"We thought of having the wedding take place outside the front porch by the knoll right before the sun goes down. It is so beautiful and peaceful. There will only be nineteen of us: Cody and family, Reid's sister and family, you, Karen, Sierra and Joe, Captain Martin, Paul, and the minister and Running Eagle. If it rains, we could all fit in the living room." Patricia's eyes were sparkling.

"Patricia and I want a simple, but beautiful wedding. And, we don't want to make too much extra work for everyone. We all should enjoy the day. I've waited a long time for this and for a while I thought it might never happen." Reid's voice was soft as he looked over at Patricia, his eyes full of love for her.

"And it shall be a wonderful day, rain or shine." Conrad smiled, "Now, you two scoot and I'll start the ball rolling. Karen, please hand me the phone and my rolodex. I'll call Father Jim now."

Reid and Patricia turned to find Running Eagle, Joe and Sierra standing by the doorway.

"You have company, Conrad." Joe announced.

Running Eagle walked into the room. "The Spirit Wind tells me to come."

Conrad glanced at everyone, "And the Spirit tells you true, my brother. Our friends wish to talk with you, and tomorrow, I ask for the healing prayer."

Running Eagle with wisdom in his eyes, nodded his head. "I will prepare for that and return at the dawn." He turned toward Reid and Patricia, "And what do you wish to talk with me about? I sense it is time you two share the wigwam."

Reid reached for Patricia's hand. "You sense correctly, Running Eagle. We would like you to give a blessing over us at the wedding. We are asking Father Jim to do the ceremony to cover the legal part and we want the blessing from you. Will you, please?"

"I will come. I shall see you both a few days before. Joining as one is important. I go now." Turning back to Conrad, "Tomorrow as the sun rises, I shall return."

And as silently as he came, Running Eagle left.

There was a feeling of peace in the room, along with the excitement of the anticipated wedding.

"You two go plan your announcement to send out, and I'll make the call to Father Jim. Sierra, come up with a few meal plans to okay with Patricia, and Joe, make sure the camera is working and there will need to be extra watchers around the lodge that weekend. Oh, and Joe, check with

Patricia on the flowers." Conrad waved his hand toward them all in a friendly dismissal and reached for the phone.

CHAPTER THIRTY-THREE

The Guests Arrive

Everyone responded to the wedding invitation. Patricia and Reid were a special couple, not being there never entered any of their minds.

Now Patricia needed to go to the city and pack up her personal belongings, talk to the property owner and make arrangements for Good Will to pick up the items she wouldn't need anymore.

She loaded up the car with clothes, music books, photo albums, personal papers, books and a few keepsakes. She was starting a new life with Reid, and they would build memories with new Christmas ornaments, pictures, and traditions.

Walking through the rooms one last time, she felt no remorse over leaving. She had lived there since her folks had died, but it never really felt like home, it had always been an apartment to her. There were no tears of regret as she gathered up her mother's wedding dress and locked the door behind her.

THE GUESTS ARRIVE

She drove over to help her brother put his things into storage just in case he didn't like the new position in Australia. He would drive back with her and spend that time at the lodge and leave the Monday after the wedding.

The next day, sitting under the shade of the big tree outside the kitchen porch, Patricia went over all the things they had accomplished and what still had to be done. She shook her head, how did people do it with hundreds of people invited to a wedding and more people in the wedding party than all of their guests.

She and Reid had driven into Durango, got their marriage licenses, and talked with the priest. She checked that off.

The meals for the weekend guests and the wedding were all planned and the food was ordered. Check.

Sierra had insisted on making the wedding cake. Check.

There was very little alteration done on the wedding dress that was hanging in the closet. Check.

Patricia couldn't believe how well everything was progressing. It helped that they didn't have any patients recovering right now.

Two more days and she would become Mrs. Reid Jones. She hugged herself. The guests were all arriving Friday sometime. No rain was forecasted, it should be a lovely day.

She looked up and saw Running Eagle standing there. She never heard him or saw him approach. She shook her head. Was she so engrossed in her thoughts not to be aware of anything around her?

Patricia quickly stood up and brushed off the back of her jeans. "Good afternoon, Running Eagle, it's so nice to see you."

"I have come to talk with you and Reid."

"Come on in, I'll get him. We were wondering when you were coming."

He gave a brief smile, "No, I would rather we talked out here." He gently lowered himself to the ground and sat with his legs crossed Indian style.

Nodding her head, Patricia went into the house and found Reid engrossed in a chess match with Conrad. Karen was sitting nearby reading.

Coming up behind Reid, Patricia put her arms around his shoulders and kissed the top of his head. "We have a visitor, sweetheart. Running Eagle wishes to speak with us outside. I asked him to come in and he said no."

Taking her hand in his, Reid kissed it. "Excuse me, Conrad, My soon to be bride and I need to confer with him. Karen, watch Conrad like a hawk so he doesn't move any of my pieces."

"My man, have no fear, I'm going to win without even trying." Conrad gave a hearty laugh. "While you two are busy, I think I will tickle the ivories." He got up and went to the piano.

As the couple walked through the house to the back, "I wonder what he has to say." Patricia asked Reid.

"Probably how the order of the service will be."

Approaching the elderly man, Reid extended his hand, "Hello my friend. We are happy to see you." Then Reid reached into his shirt pocket and took out a small bag of tobacco, which he handed to Running Eagle as a sign of respect, and shook his hand. Then he and Patricia also sat on the ground.

"I have come here today so you may prepare for your wedding in our way. Saturday morning, we will meet at sunrise here in the sweat lodge. Do you remember how you felt during and after your experience in the sweat lodge,

THE GUESTS ARRIVE

Reid?"

Reid nodded. "It is hard to put into words the newness, and joy I felt. There was a healing in my mind and soul."

"This is what I wish will happen to you both as the heat of the fire causing the steam will cleanse the body and the Spirit will take away anything that may trouble the soul, and ask the Great Spirit to be with you on your wedding day." Running Eagle paused, "Do you have any questions of me?"

"No. We do want you to give us your blessing at the end of Father Jim's talk. We feel that should be the closing of our special ceremony." Reid responded.

"Well I have a question." Patricia looked from one to the other, "What do I wear for this? I've never been in a sweat lodge before. Are we to get the teepee ready?"

"You wear something comfortable. I will have everything ready at the teepee." Running Eagle rose in one smooth move. "This is the first time that I have been asked to be part of a wedding service for non-tribal people. I am pleased that you have given me the honor to share with you at this time."

Putting his arm around Patricia, Reid spoke for both of them. "It wouldn't be complete without you. You are truly a Spiritual Leader."

Patricia nodded her head in agreement. "Won't you come in for some refreshment?" Patricia asked.

"No thank you. I will visit another time. I have others to see today." He nodded at them both and quietly walked away.

Only then did Patricia observe the horse he had tethered near the clearing. They both watched until he was no longer in sight.

***

The last couple of days before the wedding, Reid and

Patricia had spent getting the guest cabin that would be their new home, as they wanted it. Reid had been staying there since he was released from Dr. Deerwater's care. Patricia moved all of her belonging except for what she needed until the wedding. She was staying in her room at the lodge until they were married. They weren't going on a honeymoon until Ted left for Australia. They would drive him to the airport, and take a few days for themselves and enjoy some time alone.

Friday morning, Patricia was up early. Their family and guests would be arriving throughout the day. She stripped the bed, remade it with fresh linens and tidied up the room. After cleaning the bathroom, she put in some fresh soap that Sierra had made and towels that matched the shower curtain. She would be spending the night with Karen in her room, since this room was needed for guests.

A delivery truck pulled up with the flowers and fresh food. Everyone got busy and helped put them away. Karen and Patricia took the flowers to the screened in porch off the kitchen to arrange them for the rooms and wedding bouquets. The food was put into the large walk in cooler or freezer.

"I have never had so many flowers to work with," Karen stood with her hands on her hips, "I don't know where to start."

Sierra laughed softly. "I have the vases ready in the closet over there. The wrapped ones over here," she pointed to the cellophane long stemmed flowers, "Are for the wedding. Those in the buckets are for the rooms, and the others are for the corsages. You will find everything you need in that same cupboard to cut, twist, or wrap. And if you don't have enough to do, you can help make some sandwiches for us to have for lunch. I'm working on the food for the barbeque for tonight. I believe Conrad said our guests should be arriving about three o'clock."

"How come you are so prepared to work with flowers, Sierra?" Karen asked.

"Because we have so many spoiled celebrities that want flowers in their room or for their guests and we like fresh flowers in the lodge, we are prepared for just about anything. As you know, we are in the country and can't get them in the snap of the fingers."

"Oh, Sierra, are you being over worked with all of this? I thought your cousins would be here to help with the food preparations." Patricia gave her a hug.

"I'm fine, everything is on schedule and I need to keep you busy so you don't get the pre bridal jitters. My cousins will be here for tomorrow and Joe will be helping me tonight. It's all informal tonight. When your friends come, then it will be okay. It will be a time for lots of laughter and fun. Did the men get the games and things ready for the children?" Sierra's eyes had that 'I've worked with brides before look'.

"Oh yes, we will keep them entertained. And they will love the campfire tonight. We did order marshmallows, right? It's not every night we roast marshmallows." Patricia laughed.

The ladies did their magic with the flowers. The corsages were placed in the cooler, and the others in the rooms and by the fireplace. None would be put outside for the ceremony. Mother Nature was perfect enough.

They had just put things away when they heard the whirling of the helicopter. Also coming down the road was a green van and a black SUV. Everyone went to greet the guests.

Reid had his arm around Patricia and watched as the copter landed. When the blades quit whirling, the door opened, and out came Paul, Cody, Kayla and the children. Big smiles were on all their faces and big waves as they stepped down. "I'm so happy to see you! It's been so long!" Bobby Jo and Beth had their arms wrapped around Patricia. Little Andrew stood back next to Kayla. Cody was giving Reid a big bear hug.

"Man, I'm so glad you made it." Reid hugged him back; Cody was like a brother to him.

"That makes two of us! We wouldn't have missed it for anything, especially when I heard you were wearing a suit." Cody gave him a gentle hit to the arm.

Reid' sister and family left the van, as Captain Martin exited the black SUV.

Ted came around the corner and the kids were clamoring all over him. The adults were hugging and shaking hands.

"So, Patricia, are you going to introduce me to your man?" Captain Martin asked.

"Why yes. Captain Martin, my husband to be, Reid Jones. Reid, Captain Martin, a very nice man. One meets the nicest people being a nurse."

The two men shook hands. The Captain looked Reid over. He would never have recognized this man as the one he knew as Hal.

Then the men got busy and helped the pilot unload the luggage from the helicopter and from the vehicles and they entered the lodge by the front porch.

"Oh, my gosh! What a beautiful room! What a unique fireplace, and the picture above it. It's not a copy! No wonder you want to work here." Kayla turned around in a circle, taking in the living room, or the great room as it is usually referred to.

"Who plays the piano?" Betty, Reid's sister asked.

"Dr. Deerwater, Reid, myself, and I think the twins are taking lessons." Patricia answered.

"Maybe we can have a sing-along later." Betty thought aloud.

"Anything is possible, we don't have any plans after the barbeque and the kids roast some marshmallows." Patricia smiled at her.

Joe and Sierra stood quietly watching everyone interact, and were joined by Karen and Dr. Deerwater. The kids were racing around outside with Ted, burning off some energy after their long rides.

With his baritone voice, Dr. Deerwater got the visitors attention. "Welcome everyone to my lodge. I am Dr. Deerwater, but please call me Conrad. I hope you enjoy your stay here as we celebrate two of my favorite people unite in marriage and become as one."

There was clapping of hands and from the doorway, Ted gave a whistle. The children jumped up and down and clapped their hands too. Reid leaned over and gave a blushing Patricia a kiss.

Dr. Deerwater continued, "If you need anything, just ask. My cousins, Joe and Sierra will assist you. Joe is also a licensed physical therapist, and Sierra a registered dietician. So, if any are in need of a back rub, or a special cup of tea, just ask. Paul is a doctor, and Karen and Patricia are nurses, so we are prepared to treat anything." Conrad smiled at them all and sat down in the deep chair by the fireplace.

Sierra stepped forward, "If you will follow Joe and me, we will show you to your rooms.

There was a flurry as parents corralled their children to see where their rooms would be.

Conrad comfortable in his chair listened to the normal sounds of people getting settled in their rooms, and admonitions to the children to be quiet. He had never had time to think about marriage himself, what with his working hard to become a plastic surgeon, build the lodge and help those on the reservation.

But now, he looked around the great room, and he could envision Karen sitting with him watching a toddler or two playing there. Would she consider that? Did she feel the same about him? He sighed. Tomorrow was the big day for Reid and Patricia, then there would be time for Karen and him to see if their lives could entwine as one.

"A penny for your thoughts," A smiling Karen looked down at Conrad. "Or maybe you would just settle for this cold glass of lemonade."

Conrad stood up and motioned to the couch. "Come sit with me." He took the offered glass from her.

When they were both seated and took a drink, Conrad spoke, "Thank you so much for thinking of me. This lemonade hits the spot."

"I think of you and your comfort a lot, Conrad and not just as a nurse." She smiled at him.

"And I think of you often, and not as a doctor." Conrad leaned closer to her, Karen leaned closer to him, and their lips met in the middle.

Reid and Patricia walking down the hallway, noticed the couple kissing. Patricia couldn't help herself, "Karen is that the new way of taking a temperature?" And laughing she and Reid went out on the porch.

Conrad put his and Karen's glasses on the table, settled back and putting his arms around her, "I think we should check the blood pressure now too," and proceeded to share another warm kiss.

CHAPTER THIRTY-FOUR

Man Talk

Ted and Dave were playing ring toss with the children in the back, little Andrew was sleeping in his mother's arms and the other ladies were keeping her company as they discussed how the kids had grown, and their many activities. Conrad was in his room resting.

"How about giving me a small tour around this wonderful lodge?" Capt. Martin said with a wave of his arm.

"I'd be glad to. Care to join us Cody?" Reid looked over Cody who was sitting in the chair with his hands laced behind his head.

You bet. If I don't move, I'll be taking a nap." He smiled as he slowly stood up and stretched.

The men went down the steps and ambled toward the garage area, talking about cars.

Our of ear shot of anyone, Capt. Martin changed the subject. "I didn't recognize you at all when I saw you, Reid. The fact that you are alive is a miracle. I wish I had never asked you to go on that last stakeout." The last words came out hoarse. He shook his head, "You both always did your best. I never doubted that you two wouldn't complete an assignment. You made a great team." He shook his head slowly then looked up at Reid. "We didn't have an escape route. We slipped up on this one, big time. Just having our gal as a waitress wasn't enough. We should have had the place bugged and one of our men renting a room across the street. I'm truly sorry, Hal, I mean, Reid."

"Captain, actually, this all ended for the best, I know that sounds weird. In saving my life and repairing my face, Dr. Deerwater gave me the new identity that makes me safe. If you didn't recognize me, neither will any of the scumbags that I've arrested." He stopped and looked around, a force of habit from years of undercover work.

"I hate to admit it, but that last job affected me terribly. My body was healing and I was doing the entire PT that I was required to do, but mentally, I was a basket case. I had such terrible nightmares. I kept reliving the beating over and over again. During the day, I was pretty good. Patricia was my nurse, not knowing I was really Hal. It was getting harder to keep it from her. I was afraid of everything. There are Indian people that constantly patrol the grounds. Don't look, you won't see them. Conrad has them on the payroll because all the movie stars and politicians that he does plastic surgery on need privacy and not the news media around. The lodge is on the reservation and the Indians do carry guns."

Reid adjusted his Stetson and continued, "Patricia and I did so much together and one night we were playing music from the movie OKALAHOMA, we had done that on the piano with two hands when I was Hal, and it seemed so right. As we slowly walked back to my room, I hugged her and my heart was breaking. That night I had a dozy of a nightmare.

Joe, the physical therapist, had Sierra make me some tea and suggested I visit with his medicine man, Running Eagle. Which I did."

"I read the report, I'm so sorry, Reid." The captain looked at Reid with tears in his eyes. "How did this man help you?"

"He talked with me, gave me a dream catcher to put in my window and told me the Indian belief that it would catch the bad dreams and only let the good ones through. We went into the sweat lodge and he prayed for me and something dramatic happened in there. The Lord, Holy Spirit, Great Spirit, God, whatever name you give the Higher Power, touched me that day. I felt like lightning went through me. I haven't had nightmares since. Every day, I thank God and praise Him for that and everything I have and do."

"Wow that is powerful! No wonder you don't want to leave this place. I felt peace the moment I got out of my SUV. So, is that when you told Patricia who you were?"

"Well, Captain, I guess I took that out of his hands." Cody spoke up for the first time. "I had sent Reid a letter with pictures of my family. Patricia saw it on the dresser. At first she was angry because he didn't tell her who he was right away, then just extremely happy that he was alive. She had been having feelings toward Reid like those she had with Hal, but felt unfaithful in a way, not knowing if Hal was dead or not. She never felt he had died."

Reid interjected, "Then when it was all out in the open, we were free to rekindle that love we have had for each other and I asked her to marry me. She knows that life will never be the same; we have to reinvent our past life when we move from here so we can have other friends. But we have each other. Well, legally and spiritually when we tie the knot tomorrow." Reid laughed.

"So, we have what can be called a happy ending here. That's great!" The captain rubbed his hands together. "Now what are your future plans?"

"For the time being, I will stay on as caretaker, help Joe out a bit, and Patricia is going to be the nurse here for patients. We plan on helping Conrad however he needs us since he is going to do more free surgeries on his people here on the reservation. When we aren't needed here, we are free to go on short trips or whatever. If we want to move on, we can, but I know Patricia wants to stay in the nursing field. Plus, when I paid for her education, I put in the stipulations that after she received her nursing degree, she helps someone else, not necessarily in the nursing field. She still wants to do that." Reid smiled at the two men. "I am very happy, and after tomorrow, I won't be alone any more either."

The women on the porch saw the three men in a hug. "They must be bonding, like the football team." Karen commented. They all laughed.

Sierra stepped onto the porch. "Ladies, when would you all like to eat? Conrad thought in about fifteen minutes. Would that be acceptable with you?"

Patricia stood up, "Perfect. What can I do to help?"

Smiling, Sierra replied, "You have the hard task, getting the children rounded up and hands washed. I have set things out in the screened porch."

Patricia was spared running after them as the children all came trooping in with cries of, "We're hungry."

"That's what we wanted to hear. Everyone go and get washed up for dinner and we will meet in the screened porch off the kitchen. I'll go get the men." Patricia went down the steps and toward the men.

When she was within shouting range, "Dinner is ready. Come and get it or we'll throw it out!"

The men turned and started to jog toward the house. "Save some for me, I'm starving." Cody yelled out.

And the race was on as the three men couldn't pass up a challenge. It was a draw as they reached the porch.

But, Reid was the only one that was met with a kiss. In Patricia's eye, he was the winner.

CHAPTER THIRTY-FIVE

The Wedding

It was still dark as Reid gently tapped on Karen's door. Patricia opened it quickly with a "Shush."

They shared a kiss and quietly walked down the dimly lit hallway. Running Eagle had said sunrise and it would soon be here.

"Do you believe in the old saying about not seeing the bride on the wedding day before the wedding ceremony?" Patricia whispered to Reid.

"No. Only if the bride was really ugly and it was an arranged marriage and the groom would be the one to run away." He quietly laughed back.

"Or, he was really nasty and mean looking, but her dad had paid a huge dowry and she would refuse to marry him." Patricia gave him a sidewise glance.

Reid caught her in his arms and held her tight. "Never fear my darling. You are the most beautiful woman in the world. When my eyes were bandaged and I couldn't see, I knew you were there, beautiful inside and out." He leaned down and kissed her ever so gently.

"Ahem, the fire is ready to put the water on and mother sun is just about to come over the mountain." Running Eagle's voice startled them.

"Good morning, Running Eagle. Did you sleep at all last night? You would have to get up very early to travel here and get the preparations finished." Patricia asked.

"No, I didn't sleep. I sent out prayers to the Spirits for this service and your wedding. Old men don't need much sleep. Come." He led the way.

Patricia and Reid exchanged looks.

At the entry of the tent, Running Eagle removed his moccasins, and Patricia and Reid followed suit. Bending down, they entered the sweat lodge.

Patricia was almost overwhelmed with the heat.

"You have the tobacco, Reid?"

"Yes." Reid handed the small leather bag to Running Eagle.

Running Eagle took the pouch of tobacco and had Reid pour a cup of water from the pail on to the hot stones causing more steam which made the tent get even hotter.

Running Eagle chanted in his language as they walked slowly to the right in a circle around the fire. After a few minutes, he stopped. "Sit."

Taking a pinch of tobacco, he sprinkled it to the north.

"Holy Spirit, we pray for this young couple that anything they carry within themselves that is unholy or unhealthy, we ask you to take away from them."

He stretched his hand to the east releasing another bit of tobacco, chanting, "Holy Spirit of the morning, let each sunrise be a new beginning that will renew their love."

Turning to the south, as the tobacco left his fingers,

"Holy Spirit of the south, may their lodge always be safe and they have enough food to share."

To the west, he released more tobacco from his fingers, "Holy Spirit of the west may their home have the blessing of a child to nourish and love."

Running Eagle bent and put another cup of water on the coals causing them to hiss and send out more steam.

Patricia was surprised she was still able to breathe with all the heat.

"Pray to the Spirit you believe in, aloud or silently. Pray for your blessing." Running Eagle instructed as he picked up a small old wooden drum with tanned stained hide stretched over it. Using a small wood stick with a carved wood ball on the end he began to drum, praying out loud.

Reid and Patricia also said their prayers, but quietly, each in their own way. The power of God filled the tent as they asked for forgiveness of any sins, to cleanse their hearts and minds of any ill feelings toward anyone, for wisdom in their choices and for their union to be blessed.

Tears rolled down their cheeks mingling with the sweat. They were overwhelmed with joy and a feeling of freedom.

The drumming stopped. The three people sat in silence absorbing the peace.

Silently, Running Eagle rose, bending down, left the tent to be greeted by the morning sun. Reid gave Patricia a hand to help her up and they followed.

Running Eagle touched Reid's arm, then Patricia's. "Faith in the family is good. I will see you this afternoon for the wedding."

"Thank you for this morning. You will speak after Father Jim to give the final blessing. Until then…" Reid shook his hand, and Patricia gave the old gentlemen a hug.

THE WEDDING

They stood arm and arm as Running Eagle was ready to put his foot in the stirrup to mount his old horse when Father Jim, Joe and Sierra walked quickly toward them.

"Wait! Running Eagle." Joe called out. "Don't leave."

Father Jim spoke rapidly, "I have received some bad news that the priest who is my mentor was badly injured and may not survive. He has asked for me. I need to leave now. I was wondering if we could do your marriage vows now. There isn't time to find someone to fill in." Father Jim was clearly upset.

Reid and Patricia looked at each other. Both nodded yes.

"Father, can you give us fifteen minutes so our friends who have traveled so far can witness us taking our vows?" Patricia asked quietly.

"Yes, I can do that. Where would you like the service to be?"

"Right here," she replied.

Running Eagle nodded and getting off his horse looked over at Joe, "Better wake up Conrad."

In twenty minutes, everyone was present in various states of dress. The children were still in their pajamas, the women in the skirts and tops they were going to wear, and the men in jeans and clean shirts.

Then, Patricia, her hair still wet from a quick shower, wearing her mother's wedding dress, her arm entwined with her brother, walked gracefully in the long white dress, stopping in front of Father Jim and Running Eagle.

Reid had sucked in his breath as he watch her and Ted come toward them. She looked radiant, so beautiful. He smiled that smile that only a man deeply in love can, and stepped next to her.

"Friends and family of Reid and Patricia, I welcome

you to witness and celebrate the joyful uniting of a man and woman whose care, affections and understanding have flowered into a deep and abiding love."

Father Jim looked over at Ted. "Who gives this woman in marriage?"

Smiling, Ted waved his arm to include the entire small group, "Her friends and I do."

Lifting up her veil, he kissed her on the cheek and placed her hand on Reid's.

Father Jim began, "No ceremony can create your marriage; only you can do that, through love, patience, dedication, perseverance, through talking and listening and trying to understand each other."

"Help and support one another through tenderness and laughter, co-operation and play, through learning to forgive, and learning to respect and appreciate your differences and to make the important things matter and to let go of the rest."

"Join your hands. Do you, Reid, promise to love and support Patricia, honor, adore and cherish her all the days of your life?"

"I do, with all my heart." Reid answered, his eyes never leaving Patricia's face.

"And you, Patricia. Do you promise to love and support Reid, offering your friendship and loving care, adore and cherish him all the days of your life?"

"Oh, yes, I do." Patricia said in a quiet voice.

"What token do you have of your love for each other?"

Cody stepped forward and handed the priest two gold rings.

"The wedding ring has been the traditional symbol of commitment and enduring love, because, as a circle, it is without beginning and without end. It is the endless love that links you spirit to spirit."

Handing the small ring to Reid, "Reid, place this ring on Patricia's finger and repeat after me: 'this ring is the symbol of my unconditional love and support'."

Reid repeated it in a clear voice and put the ring on her finger, raised her hand and kissed it.

"Patricia, place this ring on Reid's finger and repeat after me; 'This ring is the symbol of my unconditional love and support'."

She too repeated the words and slid the wider plain band of gold on his finger, smiling at him.

"In as much as Reid and Patricia have agreed to these vows, by the power vested in me by the State of Colorado, and the church, I now pronounce you husband and wife."

As Father Jim took a step back, Running Eagle stepped forward.

Running Eagle removed two pieces of red ribbon from his vest pocket and tied one around Reid's wrist, and one around Patricia's wrist. Then he joined the ends of Reid's and Patricia's together.

He spoke slowly so the words would be special.

"I have joined you together with the ribbon in my people's way just as Father Jim used the rings. My young friends, I share with you an ancient Indian benediction:

Now you will feel no cold, for each of you will be warmth to the other.

Now you will feel no pain, for each will be comfort to the other.

Now there is no more loneliness for each of you will be companion to the other.

Now you are two bodies, but there is only one life before you as you go now to your dwelling place to enter into the days of your togetherness."

"Go forth, with your God, in peace and joy all the days

of your life. This blessing upon your union is a perfect beginning of a new life of love and adventure."

"And now in the custom of your people, you may kiss."

And they did.

The End

ABOUT THE AUTHOR

Donna Bryan was born and raised in La Crosse, Wisconsin. She has also lived in Minnesota and Missouri with her family. Throughout these moves, she has always enjoyed writing articles, worship services, children's stories, and programs.

It wasn't until Donna retired, that her children insisted she publish her stories. Her first book, *Truck Drivin' Man: Warrior of the Road*, was followed by *The Mansion: Discovering More Than Just an Inheritance*.

While visiting her three sons and grandchildren in Colorado, a lion was seen dragging a deer across the road just yards from the home she was staying at. The story of the lion meant to be a two page story for her grandchildren kept growing and became *Spirit of the Mountain: The Lion - The Ranger - The Journalist*.

Her book for children, *The Olympian Cat Arthur* was published at the time of the 2014 Winter Olympics. That was followed by Donna's most recent story: *The Cabin, The Nurse, Life Changes*.

Donna hopes you enjoy reading her books as much as she did writing them. More about Donna and her latest writing projects can be found at: www.DonnaMBryan.com.

OTHER BOOKS BY DONNA M BRYAN

Truck Drivin' Man:
Warrior of the Road

Jack is a Christian truck driver who has many exciting experiences as he travels across the United States helping others.

THE MANSION:
Discovering More Than Just An Inheritance

Ben discovers he is the sole recipient of his grandfather's will. He also discovers JC is a policewoman. As he takes possession of the mansion, can he also take possession of her heart?

SPIRIT OF THE MOUNTAIN:
The Lion - The Ranger - The Journalist
Mystery, adventure, suspense and romance awaits in Spirit of the Mountain.

The Olympian Cat Arthur
Arthur lives at the stadium as the official mouse detective. Arthur has watched many skaters and is determined that he can skate too. With a little help from his friend, Marla, the magic happens.